the romantic comedies

W9-BGD-864

Love on Cue

CATHERINE HAPKA

Simon Pulse

New York London Toronto Sydney

This book is a work of fiction. Any references to historical events, real people, or real locales are used fictitiously. Other names, characters, places, and incidents are the product of the author's imagination, and any resemblance to actual events or locales or persons, living or dead, is entirely coincidental.

SIMON PULSE
An imprint of Simon & Schuster Children's Publishing Division
1230 Avenue of the Americas, New York, NY 10020
Copyright © 2009 by Catherine Hapka
All rights reserved, including the right of reproduction in whole or in part in any form.
SIMON PULSE and colophon are registered trademarks of Simon & Schuster, Inc.
Designed by Ann Zeak
The text of this book was set in Garamond 3.
Manufactured in the United States of America
First Simon Pulse paperback edition April 2009
10 9 8 7 6 5 4 3 2 1
Library of Congress Control Number 2008934750
ISBN-13: 978-1-4169-6857-3
ISBN-10: 1-4169-6857-1

One

"O Romeo, Romeo! wherefore art thou Romeo? Deny thy father and refuse thy name; Or, if thou wilt not, be but sworn my love, And I'll no longer be a Capulet!"

As I uttered Shakespeare's immortal words, I felt my heart swelling with emotion. Acting does that to me. Most of the time I'm not the type of person to, well, emote. Or even to talk that much. At least not in public. I get tongue-tied just speaking to strangers, and telling me I have to give a report in front of the class is like telling me I have to face a firing squad. Worse, actually. At least with the firing squad it's all over quickly. Basically, if you asked my friends and family to come up with three words to describe me, "shy" and/or "quiet" would definitely be in there somewhere.

Somehow, though, all it takes is to put me onstage under the lights (or even in Nico Vasquez's basement rec room goofing off Shakespeare-style with my friend Duane Clayton in front of the rest of the high school drama club, the Thornton Thespians) and *poof!* I'm no longer regular old Maggie Tannery, ordinary high school junior and life-long Quiet Girl. Instead, I'm more like the Maggie that I am inside my head, an International Maggie of Mystery with no inhibitions and oodles of wit and charisma. I'm able to just *become* whatever character I'm playing; free to say whatever she would say, do whatever she would do, feel whatever she would feel. At that moment, for instance, I felt my lips quiver and tears glisten in my eyes as I gazed up into Romeo's—er, Duane's—face, thirstily drinking in the very sight of him.

"I take thee at thy word." Duane swept back his floppy brown hair and bowed before me, his eyes locked on mine. "Call me but love, and I'll be new baptiz'd; Henceforth I never will be Romeo."

I took a step closer and clutched his hand in mine. "What man art thou that thus bescreen'd in night, So stumblest on my counsel?" I cried.

Duane rolled his eyes. "Duh. Didst thou hearest me not? I saideth my name is Romeo. Be-eth thou blind? Dude you fell in love with earlier, remember?"

I giggled, the spell broken. Leave it to Duane!

"I knowest thou art not my Romeo," I said, doing my best to keep a straight face as snickers came from the direction of our audience, which consisted of about a dozen of our fellow Thespians. "For my true love Romeo wouldst not speaketh to me thusly. Thou must be some malicious imposter, determined to trick me with thy dorkitude."

"Alack!" Duane cried, clutching both hands to his heart. "Thou woundest me with thy sharp words. In fact, thy words are so sharp that I bleedeth, I die-eth . . ." He staggered a few steps, moaning and groaning with great enthusiasm. Collapsing onto one knee, he keeled over and thrashed on the floor. I'm not sure you could call it Method acting. More like channeling Scooby-Doo.

"Hey! Watch the equipment, man." Nico hurried forward to pull his guitar stand and one of his speakers out of the way of Duane's vigorous death spasms. Nico's basement could probably qualify as a professional-level recording studio, with speakers, amps, all kinds of instruments from keyboards to a cello, and a bunch of other equipment I didn't even recognize.

Everyone else was laughing by now. "Alack," I exclaimed, putting one hand to my forehead like a silent movie actress about to be tied to train tracks. If there's one thing more fun than acting, it's *over*-acting. "My true love hath met his untimely end. Oh well—more fish in the sea and all that." I sashayed over to Nico as he set down his speaker and brushed off his hands on his black jeans. "Hey, big boy. Art thou perchance seeking a damsel of thine own?"

Nico rolled his eyes. "Very funny," he muttered, casting a worried eye at a microphone stand near Duane's thrashing legs. Duane is almost six-and-a-half feet tall, so he covers a lot of ground when he's sideways.

I took a bow as the audience applauded and shouted encouragement and Duane continued to flop around on the floor like an oversize fish in baggy cargo pants. My best friend, Calla Markov, stood up and pumped one fist in the air.

"You go, girl!" she cried. "That's how old Willie S. should have written it in the first place. Why should Juliet kill herself just 'cause Romeo's an impulsive spaz?"

"Well, it *is* supposed to be a tragedy," one of the Paolini twins pointed out.

"Whatever." Calla rolled her eyes. "All I can say is, it's pretty obvious that *Romeo and Juliet* was written by a man."

"Let me guess, Calla. Does that mean you won't be trying out for Juliet in the spring play?" Nico asked as he grabbed the microphone stand. A couple of the guys were still egging Duane on in his death throes, which now resembled a grand mal seizure.

Calla shrugged and batted her fake eyelashes at Nico dramatically. Calla does *everything* dramatically. "Why bother?" she said. "Everyone knows fat girls don't get cast as Juliet."

"Don't be ridiculous," I told her. The whole "fat girl" thing was part of Calla's schtick—always had been—but that didn't mean I had to like it. "You should totally try out for Juliet. I think you could bring a lot to the part."

I winced, realizing a split second too late that I'd set her up perfectly. I have a way of

5

doing that. She says I'm just a natural-born straight man.

"Oh, I sure would, honey." She grinned and patted her upswept hair, which was platinum blond this week and secured with a couple of red lacquered chopsticks. Then she did what she calls her boom-boom move, swinging her ample hips from side to side so her beaded skirt shimmied. "I would bring a *lot* to the part."

Nico let out a snort, then turned and wandered off. I watched him go, hoping he didn't regret agreeing to host the Thespians' traditional last-night-of-spring-break party this year. Normally we had trouble convincing him even to come to our parties, though he'd mixed the sound for every production since freshman year.

As Thornton High School's resident quirky, sarcastic musical genius, Nico wasn't exactly your typical theater geek. With his spiky black hair and punk-rock attitude, he was way too cool for the rest of us. Still, to judge by the amount of time he spent hanging around making sardonic quips, he didn't seem to mind too much. Sometimes I wondered exactly why he bothered spending so much time with the Thespians. It wasn't as if his job as sound man required him to attend every meeting. Calla always said it was because he harbored a secret desire to be a theater geek himself. But I'd invented a few more interesting reasons inside my head. For instance, maybe Nico was hanging out with us as part of some undercover alien study of the habits of human youth. If I were to write out that theory as a play, it might go something like this:

GLARG FROM PLANET BLOOP: Report, minion! Of what activities have the young humans been partaking during this latest lunar cycle?

NICO: It is very strange, Commander Glarg. They stand upon a wooden platform and recite the same words over and over while flailing about in a series of movements. They call it "acting."

GFPB: How peculiar. This primitive race never ceases to cause my brain synapses to quiver with confusion.

NICO: I concur. Their grooming habits are also most odd. For instance, to maintain my humanoid disguise, I must apply a strangely perfumed, gelatinous substance to the fibers growing from my humanoid scalp. The human creatures refer to it as "hair gel." While the odor of it is somewhat pleasant, it is causing my antennae to go soft.

GFPB: Extraordinary!

And so on. I could amuse myself through an entire boring trig class inventing new scenarios in the much more dramatic version of life that's almost always playing inside my head. Not just involving Nico, of course. Pretty much everyone I know has starred in my little dramas, including me. When I was younger I used to imagine my future fabulous life as a pop star or an international photojournalist, even though the chance I'd ever become either was less than zero. Still, inside my head it didn't matter. I could be as bold, brave, outgoing, sexy, and talented as I could imagine, unhindered by reality or what other people might think. My little imaginary dramas are probably my biggest secret. Even Calla doesn't know how truly warped I am.

As Nico disappeared into the storage area at the far end of the basement, I flopped down on one of the lumpy suede sofas along the wall, sighing as I realized we would all be back at school in less than twelve hours. On the one hand, I definitely wasn't looking forward to cafeteria food or Ms. Horvath's killer trig quizzes. Still, there was a bright side. Tryouts for our spring production of *Romeo and Juliet* were coming up in less than a week.

"Seriously, though," I said as Calla sat down beside me, "you know Mr. Fayne doesn't go for stereotypes and stuff. He'd cast you as Juliet if he thought you had the best audition."

"Why bother? Everyone knows you're a shoo-in for the part, Mags. Even Bethany and the rest of the seniors are saying so." Calla smiled fondly at me, causing dimples to appear on both round cheeks. "You proved it just now. You were making magic up there—well, at least until a certain would-be Romeo forgot his lines and started goofing off and ruined the moment."

"Did I hear someone taking my name in vain?" Duane wandered toward us with a big grin on his long, rubbery face. I guess he'd finally finished dying while we weren't paying attention. He flung himself down onto the sofa, long legs sprawling everywhere. Throwing one arm around Calla's shoulders, he leaned over and gave her a peck on the cheek. "I never would have believed it of you, my darling."

She arched an eyebrow. "I hate to break it to you, my love. But Juliet is supposed to fall for Romeo at first sight, remember? I'm afraid you're way too goofy looking to make that believable, no matter how much pancake makeup they trowel on you. Whoever heard of a Romeo who's eight feet tall with a nose like Mount Everest?"

"Ah, but you forget." He held up one finger. "I have a secret weapon to overcome that obstacle."

"Body odor?" Calla guessed.

"No. Acting!" he cried, leaping to his feet and taking a bow.

I grinned. Calla and Duane had been a couple for almost two years, ever since they'd played Alice and Tony in *You Can't Take It with You*. It didn't take much to picture them as one of those couples in an old black-and-white movie, trading witty banter and doing their best to entertain anyone who happened to be around. Hanging out with them sometimes, sort of, made me forget about my own completely nonexistent love life. Oh, there had been a couple of short-term boyfriends back in middle school, and early freshman year I'd had a minor thing with a kid from my English class for a couple of weeks. But all that had ended the day Derek O'Malley transferred to Thornton.

See, Derek was *perfect*. From the first time I'd laid eyes on him—his twinkling blue eyes and easy smile, his broad shoulders and long legs—he'd immediately taken on the starring role in any and all of my secret dramas that had anything to do with romance. I didn't even look at other guys anymore. What was the point? They couldn't measure up to Derek. Come to think of it, maybe that was why I identified with Juliet so easily— we were both one-guy girls. Unfortunately, unlike Juliet, my dream guy didn't return my feelings. In fact, even after two and a half years and half a dozen classes together, I wasn't sure he even knew I existed.

And no wonder. Derek was the type of guy who, up until he'd come into my life, I'd thought only existed in my imagination and in the movies. The kind of guy every other guy wanted to be and every girl wanted to be with. Mr. Three-Letter Varsity Jock,

Mr. Homecoming King, Mr. President of the Junior Class *and* the Honor Society, every girl's crush, your basic BMOC. I wondered how many of the other Thespian girls pictured Derek's handsome face to get them in the mood whenever they ran lines for romantic scenes. Hadn't I myself been doing just that a few minutes earlier while I was star-crossed loving it with Duane? I smiled, my eyes drifting shut as I imagined Derek calling up to me as I stood on a balcony, my long blond hair flowing down over my heaving bosom . . .

"Maggie. Snap out of it!"

My eyes popped open. Calla was peering into my face, looking and sounding slightly exasperated. Oops. Apparently I'd slipped into a fantasy about Derek while my friends were talking. It happens.

"Sorry," I said. "What were you saying?"

Calla rolled her eyes. "Let me guess. Judging by the sappy expression on your face, you must've been daydreaming about Mr. Perfect, right? Either that or those tacos we had for dinner gave you indigestion."

Like I said, Calla doesn't know about my secret dramas. But she *does* know all about my monster crush on Derek.

"Give her a break." Duane grinned and winked at me playfully. He knows too. "Every great actress has to draw on powerful emotions if she wants to connect with the audience. It's not like she'd be convincing as lovelorn Juliet if all she had to think about was boring old me, right?"

"You do have a point there," Calla agreed.

I smiled weakly. In a way they were right—my intense but hopeless crush had fueled more than one passionate performance onstage over the past couple of years.

However, I gladly would have traded all my possible future Oscar nominations for just one real-life adoring, Romeo-esque glance from Derek.

Two

"Coming through." Nico reappeared, carrying a big, boxy piece of equipment dragging an extension cord. He stepped over Duane's feet, heading toward the "stage" where we'd been acting, which was actually just a corner of the basement.

"Ooh, karaoke?" Calla's jade green eyes lit up. "I hope you have some Janis Joplin. I feel like belting it out old-school."

"Your wish is my command." Nico shot her his crooked half smile before continuing on his way.

"What about you, Mags?" Duane asked, reaching around Calla to poke me on the shoulder. "Are you going to regale us with some operatic arias or something?"

I stuck out my tongue at him. "Dream on. You know I don't sing."

"You've come a long way, Mags." Calla gave a throaty laugh, shaking her head. "But not quite that far, eh?"

Calla and I had been friends practically since birth, so she'd known me before I became a theater girl. All through elementary and middle school people called us the Oppies, because we were opposites in just about every way. She was tall and plump, I was short and thin. She had dark eyes and dark hair (at least until she started dyeing it), while I was blond with a fair complexion. But most of all, she never stopped talking and wasn't afraid of anything, while I was so shy and self-conscious that some people probably thought I was mute or something. I still suspect that was why we became such close friends in the first place. Calla is a natural-born caretaker, loyal and protective, and I think our friendship started off as sort of a project for her—not that she'd admit it now.

Meanwhile my parents never knew quite what to do with me. Both of them are outgoing people themselves and were clearly troubled by having such an introverted and timid daughter. If my nose hadn't been an exact replica of my mom's, and my eyes and chin identical to my dad's, they probably would have thought I'd been switched at birth, and that there was a vivacious, talkative extrovert out there somewhere trying to figure out how she got stuck with a family of bashful hermits.

By the beginning of my freshman year they were so worried, they actually sent me to a therapist for help. At first it didn't go too well. Dr. Brunner was nice enough, but when she tried to convince me to take a public-speaking class, I put my foot down. I may be shy, but I can also be stubborn!

After a while she gave up on that idea and came up with another one: the school play. Tryouts were coming up for the fall production of *The Crucible*, and she started pushing me to participate. And I was okay with that. After all, painting scenery or designing costumes counted as "participating," right?

So I showed up at auditions to sign up to be a stagehand. Thornton's drama coach happened to be Mr. Fayne, who taught freshman English and, even after only a few weeks, was already my favorite teacher ever. He's this crusty but totally lovable old man with a little white beard and a big, angular, wrinkly face that he can twist into any expression. When I told him I wanted to join the backstage crew, he sort of pursed his lips and gazed down at me, stroking his beard with his long, square-tipped fingers.

"Ah, Maggie, my child," he said in that deep, rumbly voice of his, which can pull off Shakespeare or Beckett with equal ease, "we would love to have you on the stage crew. But I have a better idea. Let's hear you read a few lines before we decide, hmm? I believe you'd be ideal for the role of Mary Warren. It's a very small part—just a handful of lines here and there—but I believe it might suit you well. How about it?"

For a second my stubbornness welled up and I started to shake my head—thanks, but no thanks. Somehow, though, looking into those wise, watery blue eyes, I couldn't refuse to do what he asked. What harm was there in humoring him? He would see how hopelessly bad I was as soon as I opened my mouth. Tryouts had just started and not many people were there yet, so I figured it shouldn't be any more embarrassing than the typical oral report, and I'd survived plenty of those. Besides, trying out for an actual speaking role was pretty much guaranteed to get my parents and Dr. Brunner off my back, even if I didn't get cast. Calla was there auditioning, and she volunteered to read with me, and just like that I was committed to giving it a try.

So I climbed up onstage, script clutched in my trembling hands, and squeaked out Mary's first set of lines from the first act. Calla read the other parts, throwing herself into each of the characters with her usual enthusiasm. I responded in turn. And to my amazement . . . it wasn't that horrible! In fact, the more we read, the more I got into my part. I began to forget myself and instead imagined what it would be like to be a frightened, insecure girl at the time of the Salem witch trials. It was as if my secret imaginary life was suddenly pouring out of me and blossoming into full-color 3-D right there on the stage. As my reading grew more confident, I could see Calla glance at me now and then in surprise. But nobody was more surprised than I was. Who knew I was an actress at heart?

I landed the role of Mary Warren, and the rest is history. I discovered that whenever I was onstage, my shyness disappeared; I loved losing myself in a role and being someone else for a while, just as I'd always imagined doing. Ever since, I'd been devoted to the Thornton Thespians—and especially to Mr. Fayne. With each production, I'd taken on larger and larger roles, until this past semester, the fall of my junior year, I'd actually won the lead in our production of *The Glass Menagerie*. The show had been a huge success, and now, as Calla had pointed out, even the seniors were saying I'd probably end up playing Juliet in the spring play.

"You know, I'm glad we're doing Shakespeare this time," I mused, picking at a loose thread on the brown suede arm of the sofa. "Mr. Fayne always says you're not a real actor until you've tackled the bard."

"Yeah, it should be fun. But maybe next year we'll do *Cat on a Hot Tin Roof* so you can play your namesake, Maggie the Cat." Calla twisted her face into a playful growl and curled her fingers like claws.

"Or maybe not," I said. "I love me some Tennessee Williams and all, but Laura Wingfield was much more my speed than Maggie the Cat." We'd read both plays in English class the year before, and I shuddered at the thought of trying to play sexy, hot-blooded Maggie. Yes, I'd come a long way, but definitely not *that* far!

A few minutes later the karaoke machine was cranked up and ready to go. "Me first!" Duane said, clutching the microphone. "I think I'll begin my set with a little number I like to call 'Old Man' by Neil Young. Dedicated to Mr. Fayne, of course. Where is that cranky old bastard, anyway?"

I think everyone was starting to wonder that. Mr. Fayne always showed up at our parties for an hour or two, acting cantankerous and gruff and pretending he didn't want to be there. But everyone knew he was actually having a blast. If we were lucky, we could convince him to regale us with a Shakespearean soliloquy. If we were slightly less lucky, he might do something from Strindberg instead—occasionally in the original Swedish.

But it was after nine o'clock and he was still a no-show. "Do you think he forgot it was tonight?" I asked Calla.

"No way." She shook her head. "Since when does Mr. Fayne forget anything? He might be a million years old, but his mind is a steel trap."

I nodded, wistfulness washing over me

all of a sudden. Thinking about Mr. Fayne's age reminded me of his announcement last semester that he would be retiring at the end of the school year. The selfish part of me wished he could hold out for just one more year so he wouldn't leave until after I graduated. He'd been such an important part of my high school life so far, and it was hard to imagine finishing without him there. It was even harder to imagine anyone but him directing our plays.

But I shook off the thought. At least we had him for a few more months—and for one more play. I knew all of us were planning to make the most of it.

"Okay, forget the Neil Young," Duane said. "Crank up some 'Baby Got Back' and let me at it." He started wriggling around, doing some impromptu hip-hop dance moves. As tall and lanky as he was, the effect was something like a giant marionette being worked by a spastic child.

Nico fiddled with the controls of the karaoke machine. "Hang on, I think that one's in here somewhere . . . ," he muttered.

"Aw, come on, Duane! Can't you do a song from, like, *this* century?" Lizzy Paolini called out.

"Yeah! You're seventeen, not seventy!" Jenna Paolini added. While most of the rest of the Thespians prided ourselves on being different—okay, in some cases downright weird—the Paolini twins were the ones who kept up with current music, fashion, high school gossip, and everything else cutting-edge. They were bubbly, giggly, and cute, and with their identical wavy dark hair and curvy figures, probably fueled at least half the fantasies of Thornton's male population.

Duane ignored them. "By the way, dude?" he commented to Nico, still shimmying and shaking. "I knew you had pretty much every piece of sound equipment known to man, but I gotta say, the karaoke machine is a surprise. I didn't think you were the type to go for that."

Nico grimaced. "It's my little sister's."

"We should have known," Calla murmured to me. "God forbid Mr. Alternacool likes anything as mainstream as karaoke. We'll have to see if we can get him to entertain us all with his emo version of 'Bohemian Rhapsody.'"

I grinned. "Yeah, good luck with that. I'm sure it'll happen right after I get up there and belt out the full cast recording of *The Sound of Music*."

For the next hour, my fellow Thespians had a great time taking turns with the karaoke machine, and I had a great time cheering them on. Calla was in the middle of a full-throated rendition of a show-tunes medley when Nico suddenly reached over and turned down the volume on the machine.

"Hey." Calla frowned at him. "Is that supposed to be some kind of statement on my voice?"

"Oh, was that your voice?" Duane called out. "I thought Nico was playing with the foghorn sound effects."

Nico shook his head as Calla flipped Duane the bird. "Thought I heard someone at the door," he said. "It's probably Mr. Fayne."

"Since when does he bother to knock?" Jenna asked.

"I'll get it." Jumping to my feet, I hurried over to the door leading upstairs. I swung it open with a grin. "It's about time! We were just wondering when you'd—oh." I cut myself off as I saw who was standing there.

Not Mr. Fayne. *Definitely* not.

"Um, hi." Derek O'Malley shot me his thousand-watt smile, nearly blinding me with his perfect white teeth. "Listen, I heard the drama club was having a party here tonight. Am I in the right place?"

Three

I just stood there for a second gaping up at him in shock. Derek O'Malley. Here. At a Thespians party. Talking to me. I tried to form an answer to his question, but while my mouth moved, nothing came out. I probably looked like some kind of demented fish.

Luckily Calla came to my rescue, as usual. "Come on in, handsome," she said into her karaoke microphone. For once she managed to be somewhat subtle as she shot me a quick, amused glance—I'm sure nobody else even noticed it, though of course I started blushing anyway. "I guess you heard we throw a rockin' party and just had to check it out for yourself, huh?"

Derek stepped into the room, seeming

slightly confused. "Actually, I just wanted to talk to you guys."

I couldn't stop staring at him. Seeing him there just didn't compute. It was as if we'd been right in the middle of a performance of, say, *Arsenic and Old Lace* and suddenly Vladimir and Estragon from *Waiting for Godot* had stepped onstage and started trading existential banter. Or maybe it was more like when the car radio got stuck halfway between NPR and the Spanish-language station. No, actually, it was weirder than that. It was as if my secret daydreams had started leaking out through my ears and turning into real life. I could imagine the scientific studies now:

WORLD-FAMOUS SCIENTIST: Tell me, Ms. Tannery, when did you first suspect you could affect other people's thoughts, feelings, and behavior with the power of your mind?

ME: I remember the exact moment. It was when Derek O'Malley walked into a drama club party and declared his undying love for me.

WFS: Hmm, I see.

DEREK, TO ME: Are you almost done talking to the old coot in the white lab coat, Maggie, my beautiful darling precious sweetheart lover? Because if we don't start making out within the next thirty seconds, I shall die of a broken heart!

ME: Well, I certainly wouldn't want to be responsible for that . . . [*slurp, smooch*]

I blinked, trying to banish such thoughts. They were confusing me, and I didn't need that at the moment. I was already plenty bewildered enough. Most of the rest of the Thespians appeared to be almost as shocked as I was at Derek's unexpected entrance. And no wonder. Like every high school, Thornton had its different layers of social strata, and Derek belonged to a completely different one from the rest of us. He was practically a different species.

As usual, though, Calla was keeping her cool. "So here we are," she said. Leaning one dimpled elbow on top of Nico's largest speaker, she stared at Derek with open curiosity. "Talk to us."

Derek cleared his throat and came farther

into the room. "Right," he said. "It's like this. I went down to Mexico with some buddies for break. We did some surfing while we were down there, and somehow I managed to mess up my knee pretty bad."

"Oh, but see, when we actors say 'break a leg,' we don't mean that literally," Duane said. "So there's no need to sue us over this, okay?"

Derek laughed along with everybody else. "I know, right?" he said sheepishly. "I feel like the world's biggest idiot for doing this right before baseball season."

"I don't get it," Tommy van Cleef called out in his usual blunt way. "What's this got to do with us? It's not like we care about baseball or sports or whatever."

"Well, like I was saying, baseball season's pretty much out for me this year." Derek shrugged. "But I always thought I might like to try acting, and now it looks like I've got some time on my hands. So I wanted to find out more about what I have to do to try out for your next show."

My heart skipped a beat. Derek O'Malley wanted to be in our play? The idea was both incredible and terrifying.

Meanwhile some of the others were

looking skeptical. "You mean you hurt your knee, and now you suddenly want to be an actor?" Glenn Thalberg asked. He's a senior who has been in every production of his high school career, and he's a little protective of the Thespians.

"Let me guess," Calla added. "College apps need a bit more padding? Is that it?"

"No!" Derek said right away, shaking his head. "That's not it at all. Actually my folks think I should use this time to, you know, focus on my studies or whatever. But like I said, I've always thought acting would be fun. I've been to see almost all your shows, except during playoffs and stuff."

Wow. It was a good thing I hadn't known that at the time. It was one thing to perform in front of my friends, my family, my teachers, and everyone else I knew. But if I'd realized Derek O'Malley was sitting somewhere out in that darkened auditorium watching me, I probably would have fallen off the stage into the orchestra pit.

"Hmm." Calla crossed her arms over her chest. "He *sounds* sincere. But do we believe him?"

"I do!" Jenna Paolini put in with a giggle.

"Think about it this way, people. If he sounds sincere, it means one of two things," Rosalie Dibble spoke up, both as geeky and as logical as always. "Either he *is* sincere, or he's a good enough actor to fake it. Either way, it sounds like we should welcome him into our ranks."

"I don't know," Duane said. "If he really wants to act, maybe we ought to make him prove it—right here and now."

Nico rolled his eyes. "What's the big deal? It's an open audition, right? He doesn't need anyone's permission to try out."

"No, it's okay, man." Derek grinned. "I don't blame you guys for wanting to make sure I'm for real. What do you want me to do?"

"You may have heard our next show is *Romeo and Juliet*," Calla said. "Why don't you get up there and make like Romeo? That should let us see if you've got any chops."

There was a general murmur of agreement. "Maggie can run the lines with you," Tommy called out. "She knows the part."

Calla shot me a worried look. "No, wait, let me do it," she said quickly. "I mean, um, I want to be the one to see if Mr.

30

Smooth Talker here has what it takes." She did the boom-boom thing and fluttered her eyelashes. Most people probably thought she was flirting her plus-size butt off with Derek, but I knew the truth. She was doing it for me. She realized that if I had to get up and play a romantic scene with Derek, I'd probably faint or throw up or something.

"Don't be greedy, Calla," Lizzy Paolini cried. "You already have a boyfriend."

"Maybe she's ready to trade up," her twin sister, Jenna, joked with a sly glance at Duane, who laughed and stuck out his tongue at her. "But anyway, Maggie's probably going to end up being Juliet, so *she* should totally do it."

Calla shrugged and I gulped, feeling trapped and slightly queasy. Playing Juliet opposite Duane—or any other guy in the Thespians, or in the world, for that matter— was one thing. I could do that with both eyes shut and my script tied behind my back. But this? This was another thing entirely.

A million excuses scooted through my head. I could say my throat was sore. That I had to go to the bathroom. Or maybe I could just fake a sudden stroke. I was an actress, right? I could make it believable if I really tried. And nobody would even think about making me play Juliet in the ER.

But as usual, I wasn't able to react quickly enough to do any of those things. I just sort of froze and did nothing. And before I knew it, I found myself standing on the fake stage looking up at Derek.

At first I wasn't sure I could do it or even survive the attempt. When I gazed up into Derek's handsome face, it was as if I'd been told I had to sing "The Star Spangled Banner" stark naked in front of the entire population of Thornton High School. I just stood there, still frozen in place and feeling like I might hyperventilate. What was I supposed to do now? This wasn't how any of my daydreams about me and Derek had gone. . . .

Meanwhile he wasn't even looking at me. "Yo, cut me a little slack here, okay?" he said to the others with a laugh. "I know we studied that play back in freshman year and all, but you don't really expect me to, like, start reciting it from memory, do you?"

"Well, I suppose you *are* a beginner . . . here you go." Calla grabbed one of the scripts we'd left sitting on the speakers earlier and flipped through it. Handing it to Derek, she pointed to a spot. "Start right there, Romeo."

"Thanks." Derek glanced down at the script, then at me. The corners of his eyes crinkled in a completely adorable way as he winked and smiled. "Be gentle with me, okay?" he said softly. "I'm new to all this."

"O-okay," I managed to squeak out.

He took a deep breath and checked his script again. "Lady, by yonder blessed moon I vow, That tips with silver all these fruit-tree tops——"

"O, swear not by the moon, th' inconstant moon," I recited, my voice sounding as if it belonged to an asthmatic mouse. But somehow, in spite of the abject terror, my acting skills kicked in sort of automatically. By the second part of the line I sounded almost normal. "That monthly changes in her circled orb, Lest that thy love prove likewise variable."

"What shall I swear by?" Derek asked, his face radiating adoration. He was gazing at me as if we were the only two people in the room—in the world.

It was pretty overwhelming, but I also couldn't help being impressed. There was no trace of self-consciousness in his face or voice. He was just throwing himself into the part, bringing out the spirit of Romeo without even seeming to try. Still, he was a superstar at everything else he'd ever done. Why should it be a surprise that he could act, too?

We kept going, playing out the scene. Derek had to check his script a lot more often than I did, but he seemed to have the gist of how it went and what he was supposed to be feeling, so his lines rang true even when he stumbled over a word or phrase. And at some point everything sort of shifted, and just like that, it was as if we'd slid from reality into one of my fantasies, and the two of us really were alone beneath th' inconstant moon. . . .

"O, wilt thou leave me so unsatisfied?" he asked throatily, reaching out and taking both my hands in his.

At his touch, it was as if a jolt of electricity passed between us, leaving me almost breathless. Judging by the way his blue eyes suddenly widened, he'd felt it too.

"What satisfaction canst thou have tonight?" I asked, our eyes locked together.

"Th' exchange of thy love's faithful vow for mine." His gaze was so intense that it felt like it was burning into me, right down to my soul. Before that moment, I'd always thought "weak in the knees" was just an expression. But now I knew exactly what it meant. I wondered what he would do if I collapsed into his arms. What would it feel like to have him catch me, hold me close with those strong arms? The thought was so distracting that I almost missed my next cue.

But I managed to pull it together, reciting my next few lines even while he stared at me as if he'd just discovered the meaning of life in my face. And somehow, in turn, it was as if Juliet's words and feelings became my own and just poured out of me naturally. I forgot about the rest of the Thespians watching, forgot to be self-conscious about performing in front of my dream guy, forgot everything except expressing what I was experiencing in that moment.

"My bounty is as boundless as the sea," I told Derek with an adoring sigh. "My love as deep; the more I give to thee, the more I have, for both are infinite."

He squeezed my hands in his, leaning closer until I could smell the clean scent of his aftershave. I could practically see the sparks flying between us. This wasn't movie-star daydream secret-fantasy kid stuff. This was *real*. The most amazing part was, I was pretty sure it was mutual. The way he was looking at me . . . you couldn't fake that, could you?

"Good night, good night!" I cried at last with a touch of desperation at the thought that we were almost finished. "Parting is such sweet sorrow, That I shall say good night till it be morrow."

And just like that, all too soon, the scene was over—and so was the magic.

"So?" Derek dropped my hands and turned toward the others with a grin. "What'd you think? Was that okay?"

Most of the Thespians applauded. A couple of girls gave loud wolf whistles as well, and Rosalie let out a genteel "Huzzah!"

"Not bad, not bad at all," Duane said. "I'd say you definitely won't embarrass yourself if you try out. Auditions start Thursday after school in the auditorium."

"Cool. I'll see you all there." Derek glanced back at me and smiled. "Hey, thanks for helping out, Maggie."

I'm not sure if I managed to reply

before he left. My mind was filled with only one thought, better than all my fantasies rolled into one—he knew my name! Derek O'Malley, Mr. Perfect, my amazing Romeo, actually *knew who I was*!

Four

When I arrived at school the next morning, I was still daydreaming about repeating that sizzling love scene with Derek—over and over and over again throughout the next two months of rehearsals, with any luck.

And maybe not just onstage. I couldn't have imagined those sparks between us, could I? It was like nothing I'd ever felt before. I mean, I knew it was supposed to be a love scene, and he was acting and all, but come on—he couldn't be *that* good an actor, could he?

"Do you think he'll really try out?" I asked Calla for what had to be the twenty-eighth time since she'd picked me up in her beater of a Volkswagen.

"He seemed pretty serious about it," she replied. "And even if he wasn't totally sure he wanted to act, he definitely seemed sure he wanted *you* last night."

I grinned like a fool. "That wasn't all in my imagination, then?"

"No way. You two practically set the room on fire." Calla raised one eyebrow at me. "Frankly, I didn't know you had it in you, sweetie."

"What do you mean?"

"You know. That kind of raw passion." She snarled playfully. "The animal magnetism. Maggie the Cat!"

"Stop it." Knowing I was blushing like crazy, I let my hair fall over my face as I checked my watch. "Oops, we'd better hurry. The meeting is going to start without us."

"Let's go. I don't want to miss my chance to harass Mr. F about blowing us off last night."

We rushed down the hall and burst into Mr. Fayne's classroom. Between productions, we held drama club meetings there three mornings a week. I couldn't remember how many times I'd walked into that room, with its old silent-movie posters and framed play-bills and its wall of bookshelves stuffed with great works of literature. Usually Mr. Fayne would be leaning against the front edge of his big wooden desk, thumbing through a book or chatting with his students.

But not today. Most of our fellow Thespians were already there, but Mr. Fayne was nowhere to be seen. Instead, perched on the edge of his desk was a petite, youthful-looking dark-haired woman dressed in swishy black pants and a glittery red tank top.

"Oh my gosh!" Lizzy Paolini blurted out as Calla and I walked in. "You guys won't believe it—this is horrible!"

"Horrible!" her sister Jenna echoed.

Like many of those currently in the room, the Paolini twins could be a tad melodramatic. Hey, what do you expect? They call it drama club for a reason, after all.

"What is it?" I asked, slinging my backpack onto a free desk. I sort of automatically glanced at Nico, the *least* melodramatic person in the room.

"It's Mr. Fayne," he said simply, his dark eyes troubled.

"He's in the hospital," Duane added, hurrying toward us. His expressive face was twisted with anxiety. "A cardiac incident—that's what they called it."

"A *minor* cardiac incident," the woman at the front of the room chirped. I'd almost forgotten about her already. "Mr. Fayne will be just fine, don't you worry—especially if we all send him lots and lots of white light to help his body and spirit heal."

"Hold on." Calla held up one hand like a traffic cop. "Back up, people. Are you telling us Mr. F had a, like, a heart attack or something?"

"Or something." Nico shrugged.

"His wife took him to the hospital yesterday afternoon with chest pains," Glenn Thalberg added. "That's why he never made his grand entrance at the party last night."

"This means he's not coming back to school either," Glenn's fellow senior Bethany Cohen added grimly. "His retirement just got moved up. To right now."

I sank into the nearest chair, my whole body trembling with shock. "Oh my gosh," I whispered. It had been difficult enough to accept that Mr. Fayne wouldn't be coming back to Thornton next year. But now he wasn't coming back *this* year either?

My mind was in a fog as the dark-haired woman asked us to take our seats and then introduced herself as Ms. Dana. After assuring us again that Mr. Fayne was recovering well, she explained that she would be taking over for him as the Thespians' faculty adviser and director of the spring production.

"I know this is a big change for you, my daisies, but I believe everything happens for a reason," she said cheerfully. "So I hope you'll give me a chance."

"Wait," Tommy van Cleef blurted out. "You mean the school just, like, hired you to direct us?"

Ms. Dana laughed. "Not exactly. They actually hired me to take over Mrs. Gilbert's sophomore history classes while she's on maternity leave. But when I heard about Mr. Fayne, I immediately volunteered to do this too. The show must go on, right? You see, I'm totally devoted to the performing arts." She clasped her hands together and sighed blissfully. "There's just nothing like live theater—it's my lifeblood, my oxygen, the flowers in my meadow. I even minored in musical theater in college. I'm so thrilled and honored to step in as Mr. Fayne's understudy, so to speak."

Rosalie Dibble laughed. "Good one!" she called out. As several of us glared at her, she shrugged. "What? It was funny. Mr. Fayne would think so too."

Ignoring her, Duane raised his hand. "So what does this mean for the spring play?"

"I'm glad you asked," Ms. Dana said. "It will take me a little while to get up to speed, so I'm hoping we can start auditions the week after next. I think that's a little later than you had planned?"

"Yeah," Glenn said. "We were supposed to start this Thursday."

Rosalie raised her hand. "Even if you're not caught up, we could still run the auditions on time. All you'd have to do is show up."

"Thanks, I appreciate the offer." Ms. Dana smiled at her. "But we might as well wait. The scripts I ordered won't be in for about a week anyway."

"Scripts?" Calla glanced over at the nearest bookshelf, which held a heavy, leather-bound volume of the complete works of Shakespeare. "Why do we need scripts? We're doing *Romeo and Juliet*, right? The school already has tons of copies of that."

Ms. Dana shrugged. "Actually, I feel it might be bad karma to try to take over Mr. Fayne's show," she said. "But don't worry, I already had a wonderful idea for an alternative. Since my sophomore history classes will be studying World War II this marking period with an emphasis on the rise of the Third Reich, I thought we might bring the time period to life by staging a production of one of my favorite shows—*Cabaret*!" She swept her arms out as if taking a bow, seeming very pleased with herself.

"Oh, great," one of the sophomores muttered. "So all our rehearsals will be like History Class: The Sequel."

"*Cabaret*?" Glenn said blankly. "But wait, isn't that a musical?"

I was still struggling with the idea that Mr. Fayne was gone for good. And now, just like that, all my daydreams about the coming semester went *poof*. A musical? So much for getting together with Derek. Without the play giving us a chance to get to know each other better, he'd probably forget all about that intense moment we'd shared in Nico's basement. After all, Derek had girls throwing themselves at him all the time. Girls who weren't too shy to let him know how they felt. Girls who already knew how to handle a guy like him. Girls who didn't need any help from William Shakespeare. Girls completely *unlike* me.

"Now, I realize that *Cabaret* is a bit risqué

for a high school production," Ms. Dana was saying, seemingly unperturbed by the buzz her announcement had created among the Thespians. A few people looked as horrified as I felt. Others seemed intrigued. "But I figure that's just part of the fun, right?" She winked. "Anyway, I know we'll all have a wonderful experience together, growing and sharing and making something beautiful out of this unexpected detour on the road of life. We can dedicate our efforts to Mr. Fayne and perform our hearts out in his honor."

The buzz died down a bit. How could any of us argue with that? Then again, I couldn't help wondering what Mr. Fayne would say when he heard we were doing— *gulp*—a musical. It certainly wasn't what any of us had expected.

Especially me. I was up for just about any acting challenge, and even the idea of dancing didn't scare me—I'd taken a few years of dance classes as a kid and could hoof it with the best of them. But singing? Uh-uh. No way. Even the neighborhood cats wouldn't want to listen to my caterwauling. I didn't even sing in the shower for fear of killing Mom's spider plant, which hung in the bathroom window.

Oh well, I told myself as my dreams of epic romance wilted and died as completely as that spider plant would if I sang it the complete Beatles catalog. Maybe I could still paint sets or something. That way if Derek was in the show—and why wouldn't he be? Surely he'd be a natural at singing, just like he was at everything else—I could at least watch him from afar. That was better than nothing, right?

Five

"Well, this is a kick in the pants, huh?" Calla said as we left the room a few minutes later. "A musical. Go figure."

She didn't sound particularly upset, which was no surprise. "This could be your chance to play the lead," I said, trying to muster up a little enthusiasm on her behalf, at least. "You have a great voice—you were made for Broadway."

"Someday the world will know it, sweetie." She glanced at me. "But hang on—I hope this isn't going to be your excuse to—oh! Hi there, handsome."

I turned to see Derek loping down the hall toward us. His hair was tousled and his letterman jacket hung half off one arm.

"Aw, man, I knew it," he said breathlessly, skidding to a stop in front of us. "I missed the what-d'you-call-it meeting, right? For the play?"

"Thespians. And yeah, you did," Calla confirmed. "Better work on that, bucko. A good actor never misses a cue."

He grinned and lifted both hands in an elaborate shrug. "Hey, cut me some slack," he joked back. "I'm new at this, remember?"

The tiny part of me that wasn't totally occupied with staring at Derek was in awe of Calla. How could she just goof around with him like he was some ordinary guy? I felt my cheeks go pink as I thought back to last night, to the way he'd looked at me, the jolt I'd felt at his touch . . .

At that moment he turned toward me. "Thanks again for helping out last night, Maggie," he said. "You were awesome. You made it totally easy to get into the spirit of *R and J*, you know?"

"Um, I, wha—," I stammered hopelessly. Why, oh why, couldn't some of Calla's self-confidence and quick wit rub off on me? Better yet, why couldn't I be the better Maggie I was inside my head? Cool, calm, witty, in control of every situation . . . but no. Instead, I had to be the regular real-life me: Maggie the Spaz.

Luckily, at that moment Duane and Tommy came rushing down the hall with Nico trailing along behind them. "Dude!" Duane exclaimed, grabbing Calla by the arm so vigorously that she took a step backward. "Can you believe this? Mr. Fayne will flip when he hears we're doing a musical instead of Shakespeare. It'll probably give him a heart attack for real!"

"Hold on, what?" Derek said. "A musical? What happened to *Romeo and Juliet*?"

Duane, Calla, and Tommy all started talking at once, explaining the situation. Meanwhile Nico glanced at me.

"Weird, huh?" he said succinctly.

I just nodded. After Derek's comment, I still couldn't speak. Besides, what more was there to say? Nico had pretty much summed it up.

"So anyway," Calla finished, "it looks like *Romeo and Juliet* is out, and *Cabaret* is in."

"*Cabaret*, huh?" Derek rubbed his chin thoughtfully. "My older sister was in that show at her college. I went to see it and it was actually pretty cool. Totally dark and stuff—not like your typical silly musical."

He never ceased to amaze me. Who knew a football jock like him would know anything at all about musical theater, let alone be willing to express an opinion on it? I'd always known he was special, and this was just one more checkmark in my big mental book of proof. Or maybe one more cute little hand-drawn heart with an arrow through it in my big mental book of lu-u-u-uv. Yeah, I'm dorky like that.

Derek turned and winked at me. "And, hey—it's filled with, like, tragic love stories. So I guess our *Romeo and Juliet* practice will still come in handy, right? If we'd sung our lines to each other it would've been perfect."

Must . . . not . . . hyperventilate . . . , I thought as I smiled back at him, hoping that smile didn't look as goofy as I suspected it did.

I was once again saved from coming up with any kind of coherent verbal response, this time by a shout from Derek's football buddies, who'd just appeared at the end of the hall. He said a quick good-bye to all of us and hurried off to join them.

"Looks like Mr. Studmuffin is still planning to try out," Calla said, shooting me a look. "Interesting."

"Yeah, I gotta admit, he was pretty good last night. If he sings half as well as he acts, he's got a shot at a decent part." Duane laughed. "Speaking of which, did you guys catch a look at Glenn's face while he was up there? You could practically see him plotting Derek's murder."

"Poor Glenn." Calla shook her head, looking amused. "After his triumph as Jim in *Glass Menagerie*, he obviously thought he had the lead in the bag this time too."

"Yeah." Duane lowered his voice in imitation of Glenn's. "After all, he is a senior."

Tommy let out a snort. "Hey, at least if Glenn does end up killing Mr. Football over this part, he can use the insanity defense. There's not a jury in the country that wouldn't believe it once they got to know him."

I smiled automatically. Glenn could be kind of hard to take sometimes. On a scale of one to ten, he was probably a seven on looks and an eight on talent, but he was absolutely convinced he was a perfect eleven across the board—and he wanted everyone to know it. It had taken all my acting skills to pretend to be in love with him onstage last semester. My friends were clearly enjoying the schadenfreude of seeing his position as alpha male in the drama club suddenly challenged by Derek.

But I wasn't really focused on that. My mind was already recalculating the current situation. Trying to be logical (for a change), I laid out the facts as I saw them:

1. Derek O'Malley knew who I was (OMG! OMG!!!).
2. Derek was going to try out for *Cabaret*.
3. Derek would probably win the lead, because that was just the kind of guy he was.

All these points led to the undeniable conclusion that I had a choice to make. My options: (a) Join the stage crew. Spend the next two months staring at Derek while he rehearsed and I painted sets, like some kind of crazed, pathetic stalker; or (b) Try out for the musical myself.

Of course, that second option led to a couple of possible outcomes: (b-1) Miraculously figure out how to sing, land a real role, and live happily ever after, tra-la, tra-la; or (b-2) Get up onstage, open my mouth to try to sing, and then die of embarrassment.

Option b-2 didn't sound too great,

though I tried to find the silver lining by imagining that Derek might be the one to leap onstage to try to revive me. After all, he probably knew CPR—he was that kind of guy. Although with my luck, nerdy freshman Gary Kellaway would probably volunteer first and end up slobbering me to death.

And so the internal debate raged on through the rest of the school day, rendering me pretty much useless for anything except wandering from class to class like a zombie. It was lucky I didn't have any tests that day.

Finally I found myself walking out of the school building with Calla and Duane. They were talking about—what else?—the musical tryouts. As usual, it hadn't taken either of them long to adjust to the sudden change in plans.

"We should try to rent the movie version of *Cabaret* before auditions," Duane said. "See what we're in for. I don't even know what part I should try for!"

"Who cares? You know you'll just get cast as the weird sidekick friend or something anyway." Calla glanced over at me. "I'm more interested in hearing whether Maggie's going to try out at all."

I hesitated. "Well . . ."

"What?" Calla's eyes lit up. "Hang on, am I hearing things? Because that didn't sound like a 'hell no,' or even a regular 'no.' Are you actually thinking you might do this?"

"Don't get carried away," I said quickly. "I'm still not sure. I'm just thinking about it."

"That's a start." Calla grabbed my arm as we walked. "Listen, I know you can do this. It's mind over matter."

Duane nodded. "And hey, if it makes a difference, I heard Derek telling some of his blockheaded sports buddies about you today."

"What?" I blurted out, spinning so quickly to face him that I almost tripped over my Keds.

"Yeah. I believe the exact quote was, 'Uh, grunt grunt, me like cute Maggie actress girl, grunt grunt.' That was the gist of it, anyway."

I punched him on the shoulder. "Shut up. What did he really say?"

"Ow! You're awfully violent for a midget." He rubbed his arm. "If you must know, he told them he read the *Romeo and Juliet* stuff with you. And when one of them was like, 'Maggie who?' Derek said something like, 'You know, that cute little blonde with the turned-up nose from old Horvath's homeroom.'"

"Really?" I felt kind of lightheaded. That cute little blonde with the turned-up nose. It was practically poetry. Even Juliet herself couldn't have asked for more.

"Hmm," Calla put in. "Sounds like he's assuming you'll be trying out for the show. Just imagine how confused and disappointed he'll be if you don't."

I hesitated. It was pretty obvious they were trying to goad me into trying out— they weren't exactly the most subtle people in the world. But I knew Duane wouldn't have made up that stuff about overhearing Derek talking about me. He liked to kid around, but was painfully honest about stuff that mattered.

Besides, I couldn't help myself. I was hungry for another taste of whatever it was that I'd felt between myself and Derek last night. Maybe my unrequited love story could still have a happy ending if I just gave it a chance. . . .

"Oh well." I blew out a sigh, feeling a little flutter of anxiety in the pit of my stomach. "I suppose it's not actually physically possible to die of embarrassment, right? So what do I have to lose? You know, other than my pride, my dignity, possibly my lunch . . ."

"That's the spirit!" Duane cheered.

Calla grabbed me and yanked me into a huge hug. "I'm so proud of you, sweetie. You won't regret this—you'll see!"

"Der ish jusht one problem," I reminded her, my words muffled due to the fact that she was squishing my face into her shoulder. "I shtill can't shing, remember?"

Calla released me and tilted her head, narrowing her eyes. Since she was wearing glittery eyeliner and dark purple shadow that day, the effect was a bit eerie.

"Is it really that you *can't* sing?" she asked. "Or that you *won't* sing?"

I shrugged. "Does it matter? Either way, no sound comes out."

"I have an idea." Her eyes returned to their normal size as she smiled. "What are you doing tomorrow night?" Before I could answer, she held up her hand. "Whatever it is, cancel it. I know exactly what we have to do to get you over this problem."

Six

No matter what I did, Calla wouldn't tell me any more about her plan until we were in her car the following evening after dinner. Probably because she knew I'd back out if I had any advance warning that she was taking me to Two-Tunes-for-One Tuesday at Belters, the local karaoke bar.

"Are you kidding me?" I said as she pulled into the parking lot. "I'm not doing karaoke."

"Come on. It'll help you face your fears." She pulled into a parking spot with a squeal of tires and slammed on the brakes. Did I mention Calla drives like a drunken monkey? "Trust me, this will work."

"Doubtful." I felt a shudder pass through

me as I stared at the squat brick building with its obnoxious turquoise and fuchsia blinking sign. I was probably the only person in town who'd never set foot inside Belters. In our boring little town, it was what passed for a happening hot spot.

"Well, it's up to you." Calla opened her car door. "But unless you want to walk home, you've got to at least come inside and think about it."

What choice did I have? My house was at least five miles away, and I've never been a fan of unnecessary exercise.

"You are a cruel, cruel person," I informed Calla as we hurried for the door. She ignored me, humming scales under her breath.

When we entered the karaoke club, a kid I vaguely recognized from gym class was wailing out a nasal, slightly off-key version of some old U2 song on a little stage in front of a brick wall. I glanced around, spotting several other familiar faces in the crowd seated at the tables scattered around the room. The place looked like one of the comedy clubs I'd seen on TV.

"Hang on," I said. "There are people we know here!"

"Yeah, I mentioned to some of our

fellow Thespians that you might be doing this tonight." She smiled. "A few people said they'd come for moral support."

"Well, you'd better tell them they're wasting their time." I shook my head. "I already told you, there's no way I'm doing this."

"Fine. Go grab us a table, then. I'm going to sign myself up for a song or two. I could use the practice if I want to wow them at auditions."

She hurried off before I could answer. I sighed and turned, scanning the place for an empty table. I spotted one up near the stage and made my way toward it, weaving in between the occupied tables.

Halfway there, I felt someone poke me on the arm. Turning, I saw Nico sitting there with Tommy and the Paolini twins.

"Hey," Nico greeted me with the little twist of his mouth that passed for a smile from him. "So it's true. You made it."

"What, did Calla tell you guys you'd get to see me make a fool of myself trying to sing up there tonight?" I said with a frown. "Because if that's what you're waiting for, you might as well go home right now. She tricked me into coming here and is holding me hostage. As soon as I can wrestle her to the floor and steal her car keys, I'm out of here."

Nico looked surprised. "Oh," he said, his expression darkening to its usual who-cares gloom. "Um, she just said you might do a song tonight. No biggie."

"Yeah, chill out, Maggie." Tommy rolled his eyes. "You're such a drama queen."

I made a face at him and moved on, heading for that empty table. Calla joined me there a few minutes later, just as Jenna Paolini was finishing up a squeaky, giggly version of "Proud Mary." Yeah, it was almost as weird as it sounds.

"All signed up," Calla said cheerfully.

"That's nice," I said. Then I blinked. "Hold on. You mean *you're* all signed up, right? You didn't, like, sign me up without my permission, did you?"

"Would I do that?" She pasted a look of extreme innocence onto her face.

I frowned. "Listen, Calla . . ."

"Next up, we have Ms. Calla Markov!" the emcee, a skinny little middle-aged guy with a goatee, announced loudly. "Come on up here, Calla."

"Sorry, gotta go," Calla told me. She hurried forward and climbed onto the stage. A moment later she was belting out a full-throated version of Beyonce's most recent hit.

Sinking down in my seat, I watched her and pondered the current situation. Maybe she was right. Maybe I needed to give this a try. After all, if I couldn't sing some three-note pop song in front of a bunch of losers at a karaoke bar, how was I ever going to survive the audition process, let alone hope to land even a small role in the show so I could impress Derek with my actressy awesomeness?

So when Calla finished her song and the emcee called my name, I *didn't* run screaming from the room. Or even jump onstage and strangle Calla (though that option was tempting). Instead I stood and walked slowly and carefully up the three little steps onto the squeaky wooden boards. They felt comfortably familiar underfoot, and I imagined myself onstage at Thornton High, preparing to perform in a nice, easy, non-singing-type play.

"Everyone give Maggie a warm welcome," the emcee said, putting a hand on my back. He smelled like beer and onions. "I understand you're a karaoke virgin, Maggie."

Ignoring his slightly inappropriate leer, I nodded. My throat was too dry to say anything, even "Ew, don't touch me, you dirty old man."

"All right then, Maggie, take it away!"

He handed me a microphone and stepped offstage. I shot a panicky glance toward Calla, who had just settled herself at our table. What song was I supposed to sing? If Mr. Budweiser Breath had specified, I hadn't heard it.

The music started up. It sounded familiar. Of course, it was "My Guy," one of my favorite oldies. Calla must have hoped I'd be so nervous I'd go completely insane, forget where I was, and have a flashback to the days when the two of us used to play pop stars in my basement with a hairbrush microphone and my mom's old cassette tapes.

"You can do it, Mags!" she called up to me. I heard a few wolf whistles and cheers from elsewhere in the room, which I assumed came from other Thespians.

I say "assumed," because my entire body seemed to be frozen in place with sheer panic. That included my eyeballs, the hand clutching the microphone, and also my vocal chords. Actually, those didn't feel so much frozen as mummified and coated with a layer of dust and cobwebs.

The words to my song were popping up on the little screen at the front of the stage. I stared at it, trying to swallow past the Sahara Desert in my throat. I already knew the words. That wasn't the problem.

Calla was leaning forward. "Go, Maggie!" she hissed in a loud stage whisper. "Do it for Derek!"

A few people sitting nearby heard her and tittered. Great. Just perfect. I was well on the way to staging my own one-woman show titled *The Most Embarrassing Moment of My Life*, a.k.a. *How I Proved It Really IS Possible to Sink Through the Floor.*

A sudden flurry of movement just off-stage broke me out of my terrified stupor. To my amazement, I saw that Nico was hurrying forward. A second later he leaped up beside me, bypassing the steps. He grabbed the second microphone sitting on a stand nearby and sang out the next line of the song in a surprisingly pure, clear voice.

The place erupted into a round of applause. Under cover of the cheers, Nico leaned toward me. His breath smelled of peppermint as he whispered, "Close your eyes."

Confused, I did as he said. I was always good at taking direction—at least, that was what Mr. Fayne said.

"Now sing," Nico murmured into my ear, his breath tickling my skin.

So I did. My mouth finally opened, my vocal chords returned to life, and the notes and lyrics came out, more or less in the right places. It wasn't totally on key, and sounded more than a little shaky in spots. Not exactly ready for Broadway. But by the standards of Two-Tunes-for-One Tuesday, I guessed it probably wasn't too bad.

At the end the applause was deafening. Actually, most of that was coming from Calla. When I opened my eyes again, I saw that she'd leaped to her feet and started jumping around, screaming and whoo-hooing as loudly as she could, which was pretty darn loud. I was surprised she wasn't actually dancing on the table.

Meanwhile I turned to Nico, my hands still shaking a little. "Wow, thanks," I told him quietly. "You totally saved my butt."

He shrugged. "No biggie." Before I could say anything else, he turned and hurried offstage.

"You did it!" Calla shrieked, practically

bowling me over with a hug as I came down the steps. "I knew you could!"

"I'm glad one of us knew that." I collapsed into my seat, hardly hearing the next performer begin. "Personally, I was pretty sure I was going to die up there until Nico came to the rescue."

"Yeah, that was kind of weird. What's he doing here, anyway? I thought he hated karaoke. I only even invited him 'cause he was standing with Tommy at the time." Calla shot a quick glance toward Nico's table. Then she shrugged. "Anyway, you did it, girl! And you actually sounded pretty good doing it. See? You're not as hopeless a singer as you thought."

I pondered that, my tattered daydreams of acting bliss with Derek already stitching themselves back together in my head. Maybe Calla was right. Maybe I did have it in me, just as I did with acting, and was only waiting for the right moment to let it out. In any case, if I'd done it once, I could do it again . . . right?

The next morning we had another Thespians meeting. When Calla and I walked in, Ms. Dana was just clapping her hands for attention.

"Let's get started, shall we, people?" she cried, as peppy as an overcaffeinated cheerleader. Although I'm pretty sure no self-respecting cheerleader would appear in public wearing ankle tights, tap shoes, and a pin-striped blazer. "I have an idea for a fun exercise to start us off."

"But we're not all here yet," Rosalie called out, waving her hand in the air like the good little teacher's pet she was. "Bethany is missing, and Nico . . ."

"Never mind, they can join in when they arrive." Ms. Dana rubbed her hands together and surveyed us. "Now, I understand from talking to some of you that my little group of starlings here is new to the musical genre. So to get us in the spirit of things, I thought we could try a little exercise I call Singing Down the Lane."

She beamed at us, looking as proud as if she'd just announced she'd found a cure for cancer. She went on to explain the exercise: Each of us was supposed to sing about our goals for the rest of the semester, whether those goals had to do with the musical or otherwise. When I glanced around, I saw that most of my fellow Thespians looked somewhat dubious.

But I felt a shiver of anticipation. This would be my test. Had the karaoke performance been a fluke, or was I actually capable of singing in front of people?

"I'll start us off to give you all the idea," Ms. Dana said. She cleared her throat, then sang out, "My goal is your theatrical souls to train. And now I pass it on to . . . Duane!" She pointed at Duane, who was lounging lazily half out of his seat in the first row.

He sat up quickly, looking startled. But nothing keeps Duane off balance for long. "My goal is to learn to count to tenna," he sang in his mellow tenor voice, matching the tune she'd set but adding a few flourishes of his own. "So now I'll pass it on to Jenna."

Jenna Paolini was giggling so hard at Duane's lyric that she could hardly get out her own: "Um, I need to pass chemistry this year," she singsonged. "So now I pass to Maggie, um, my dear." Then she giggled. "Sorry, I couldn't think of anything to rhyme with your name."

I smiled at her. Then I took a deep breath. I'd just quickly worked out a lyric: *I hope Cabaret will keep me busy, now I'll pass it off to Lizzy.* All I had to do was sing it. . . .

But when I opened my mouth, nothing came out. Well, that wasn't entirely true. But what came out was less like actual human singing and more like a series of dolphinlike squeaks and scratchy yelps. I could feel my face turning red as I gulped and tried again.

"Eeyarrrrr" was about the best I could manage . . . until the door opened and Nico stepped in.

"Oh," he said. "Um, sorry. Bus was late."

Suddenly remembering his advice from the night before, I closed my eyes and took a deep breath. And just like that, my vocal chords were once again freed from their prison of terror. I sang out the lyrics I'd planned, only stumbling slightly over the name of the musical and maybe blowing the last note a little.

When I opened my eyes Nico looked kind of confused, especially when I grinned at him like a fool as Lizzy began giggling her way through her own verse. But I didn't care. I'd done it—again!

"Nicely done," Calla whispered from her seat across the aisle. "See? I knew you could do it."

I smiled at her. She'd done her part to push me to this point. But I realized now that the one I really had to thank was Nico.

A few minutes later when the bell rang, I caught up to him by the classroom door. "Hey," I greeted him, suddenly feeling shy. I mean, I'd known him for, like, three years. We were in a lot of the same classes, and of course there was the whole Thespian connection. But I wasn't sure I'd ever had a one-on-one conversation with him before. At least not a real one—the imaginary ones where he took me aside, confided that he was an undercover agent, and then told me he had solid evidence that Derek was madly in love with me didn't count.

"Hey," Nico replied. Then he shoved his hands in the pockets of his jeans and stared at me.

I swallowed hard. Okay, so he wasn't going to make this easy. Feeling my old bashfulness welling up, I tried to imagine I was some other, bolder character—maybe Lady Macbeth, or Joan of Arc.

It didn't work too well, though. It's one thing to pull off a role like that in a darkened theater in front of dozens or even hundreds of mostly anonymous people. But it turned out to be another thing entirely to do it while staring directly into Nico Vasquez's dark, intense eyes. The guy could perform laser surgery with those things.

"Listen," I blurted out, feeling my cheeks go pink. "I, uh, that tip you gave me about closing my eyes really, you know, worked. I guess."

He still didn't say anything. Just kept staring at me. It was kind of unnerving.

"So anyway," I plowed on, "I was wondering. Um, do you have any more tips like that? You know—stuff that might help me get more comfortable with singing, so I can try out for the show?"

He blinked, an expression of surprise flitting momentarily across his face. "Oh," he said. "Uh, well, I don't know."

"Oh. Okay." I felt kind of embarrassed. Since when was I so pushy, anyway? He probably had better things to do than teach me to sing. Like clean under his fingernails. Or shop for the latest in black jeans and angry-punk T-shirts. "Never mind, it's not a big deal."

I turned away, feeling any chance of getting to know Derek better slipping away like water through my fingers. Behind me, I heard Nico clear his throat.

"Wait," he said.

When I turned, he was staring at me with a weird expression on his face. Kind of like he was trying to figure out what planet I'd just landed from. Then again, maybe that was just me flashing back to Commander Glarg again.

"Look," he said. "I can teach you a few things, I guess. But I don't know how much help it'll be."

"Right now you're the only hope I've got," I told him honestly. "So thanks. I really appreciate anything you can tell me."

He shrugged. "Fine. Meet me in the music suite after school and we'll get started."

"I'll be there." I shot him a grateful smile, but he'd already spun on the heel of his black leather boot and marched off down the hall.

As I watched him go, I already felt a little better. Nico might be kind of an odd-ball, but everyone in school knew that he was the local musical expert. After all, how many other high schoolers could say they'd gone to opera camp *and* started their own punk band? If anyone could turn me into a singer by auditions next week, it was Nico.

Seven

"Keep your chin straight," Nico barked. "Don't tuck it into your neck like a turtle, or that's what you'll sound like. And relax your shoulders. You look tense."

"Tense" was an understatement. Who knew perfect posture was so important to singing? Head up, abdominals relaxed, knees loose . . . his directions were more complicated than the ones we'd had to follow when learning basic yoga in gym class the previous semester.

I took a deep breath, trying to do everything he'd said. Then I sang the same scale for about the five millionth time that day.

"La la la la la la la," I sang, keeping my

eyes squeezed shut tight. Then I opened them. "Any better?" I asked.

"A little. Try it again. This time do 'lo lo lo' instead of 'la la la.'"

I nodded and obeyed. This time when I opened my eyes, I thought for a second that he was grimacing. Then I realized it was a smile.

"That was pretty good," he said. "You know, you really don't have a bad voice, Maggie."

Before I could figure out whether that was an actual compliment, Calla stuck her head into the music room. "Yoo-hoo. Anybody home?"

"Hi. Come on in. We were just finishing up." I glanced at Nico. "Um, weren't we? You said you had to get out of here by five, and it's almost . . . oops!" I glanced at my watch. "Uh, sorry. It's like ten after."

He shrugged. "No biggie. Just meeting the guys for band rehearsal. Not like they can start without me, since I'm the lead singer." That crooked smile appeared again briefly. "See you Monday?"

"For sure." I returned his smile. "Thanks, Nico. Have a great weekend."

He nodded, then tossed a quick, sloppy

salute to Calla before hurrying out of the room. She watched him go.

"Wow, your new teacher sure is dedicated," she said as soon as he was out of earshot. "What is this, three afternoons in a row he's coached you now? You'd think a bad boy like him would have something more exciting to do on a Friday afternoon than hang out in the music suite listening to you sing scales over and over again."

"Yeah, he's been great." I started gathering up my things, stuffing the sheet music and pitch pipe Nico had lent me back into my hobo bag. "He really knows a ton of tips and stuff. I mean, I knew he was totally into music, but I had no idea he knew so much about it, you know?"

Calla smirked. "Are you sure that music is the only thing he's totally into?"

"What are you . . . ? Oh!" I frowned slightly and rolled my eyes. Like I said, Calla would fit right into an old-time romantic comedy. But sometimes, especially when it comes to romance, she concocts plot twists where even I can see that there's actually nothing but regular, boring old real life. "Get real. As if someone like Nico Vasquez would ever be interested in someone like me.

Somehow I think he goes for the more hard-core type, you know? Like, some tough-ass chick with leather pants and tattoos on her face . . . he probably thinks I'm ridiculously boring and conventional."

"Don't be so sure." She glanced off the way he'd gone. "Guys don't just selflessly spend hours helping girls they find boring."

"Trust me. I can tell when a guy likes me. *Like* likes, I mean." I flashed briefly to those magical moments with Derek last weekend, but banished the thought immediately. It was way too distracting. "Nico is being totally helpful, but like I said, if he's hopelessly devoted to anything here, it's definitely music. He's just as sarcastic and prickly toward me as ever." I shrugged. "Honestly, I can't tell quite what he thinks of me. But I don't really care. All I care about is learning to sing well enough to survive the auditions and land some kind of part, no matter how tiny."

"Eyes on the prize, right?" Calla said with a knowing nod.

I smiled, shivering as I remembered again how it had felt when Derek had gazed at me as if I were the only girl on earth. "Eyes on the prize," I agreed.

"Okay, that was halfway decent." Nico was lounging on the bench of the music room's battered old piano, leaning back against the keys. With his skinny-leg jeans, black motorcycle boots, angular cheekbones, and perfectly spiked hair, he looked like a publicity photo of a rock star. I'd been amusing myself off and on throughout our latest singing lesson by imagining a story around that—like, that he was a teenage superstar singer who was going undercover to do research on regular high school life for his first starring film role . . . but I snapped out of it when I heard his next words: "Now let's try something radical. Do it with your eyes open."

It was Monday afternoon, a little more than a week after my first session with Nico. Auditions were the following afternoon. Over the past week, Nico and I had practiced almost every day after school. He'd even helped me choose an audition song— "My Favorite Things" from *The Sound of Music*. I'd been a bit dubious at first, wondering if it might be better to do a song from *Cabaret*, since that was the show we were doing. But he'd pointed out that:

(a) "My Favorite Things" suited my range perfectly (I was willing to take his word on that); (b) I already knew most of the lyrics from seeing the movie a million times (true); and (c) it was a song I could "act" as I sang it, which might help make me more comfortable during the audition (good point).

So we were going with his suggestion, and I'd practiced it until I knew it backward and forward. (Literally. Just for fun, I'd tried singing it backward one day in the shower. I made it all the way through, and better yet, the spider plant survived.)

But now that the big day was almost here, I had a nervous flutter in the pit of my stomach. Okay, maybe more than a flutter. It felt as if a pterodactyl was loose in there.

I'd felt a bit better as soon as I walked into the music room and saw Nico waiting for me there on the piano bench. There was something reassuring about knowing he'd heard me at my worst and hadn't gone deaf yet.

But now he was throwing me for a loop. "Eyes open," I repeated uncertainly. "Um, are you sure that's a good idea?"

"Yeah, I think it's an excellent idea," he said drily. "Unless you were planning to audition tomorrow with your eyes closed."

Actually, that was pretty much exactly what I was planning. Even with all the coaching and extra practice, I wasn't expecting any miracles here. With any luck I'd wind up with a small part—minimal singing, no solos, but just enough stage time to cozy up to Derek a little.

I wasn't sure Nico would appreciate that line of reasoning, though. Anyway, I'd been making pretty good progress the past few days, so I figured his suggestion was worth a try. He twisted around and tapped out my first note on the piano, and I took a deep breath. My eyes started to flutter shut of their own accord.

"No!" Nico barked. "Open. Go."

I gulped and forced my eyes wide again, not daring even to blink. "Raindrops on roses . . . ," I began.

But this time the notes were all over the place. My voice wobbled like crazy. I sounded like a cat in heat. A tone-deaf cat. With a sore throat.

"Ugh!" I cried, quitting after two lines. "That totally sucked!"

"Yeah. It wasn't pretty." He swung around on the bench and stood up. Stepping toward me, he added, "Let's try something else. Look at me."

"Uh, isn't that what I'm already doing?" I joked weakly, still kind of distracted by my own suckitude.

"No. I mean *look* at me." He grabbed my arms and positioned me so I was facing him directly.

I blinked, startled by his touch. Nico wasn't what you'd call a touchy-feely person. Come to think of it, neither was I.

Staring at him at such close range, I noticed his olive-tinged skin was as smooth and perfect as a model's in the "after" part of a zit-cream ad. He was so close that I could feel his warm breath on my face and smell that hint of peppermint I'd noticed before— toothpaste? Gum? Meanwhile he was staring directly into my eyes with those intense, dark brown laser beams of his.

"Okay," he said in a low, gruff voice. "*Now* sing."

"Wha . . . I . . . huh?" I burbled, too dazed to form coherent words.

"Sing!" he barked. "Raindrops on roses . . ."

He went on to sing the first couple of lines of the song. Even in the midst of my confuzzled state, I couldn't help being impressed by his perfect pitch and the way his voice sort of changed, losing its grit and turning honey smooth, embracing the wholesomeness of the song. That distracted me from my own fears just enough for me to join in, picking up the song on the third line. Staring into his face, I ended up singing the rest of the verse and the first chorus. By the end, Nico was smiling. He leaned forward slightly, and for one crazy moment I thought he was going to kiss me. Calla's comments about him liking me raced through my head. Could she be right?

But a second later, to my relief, Nico dropped his grip on me and took a step back. "There," he said. "That was better."

I realized he was right. Actually, "better" was an understatement. My voice had sounded strong and sure, holding its own beside his. There had been no hesitations, no bum notes. It was definitely the best I'd ever done—with my eyes open, at least.

"Thanks!" I blurted out. I was still kind of weirded out by his method, especially that bizarre moment at the end. But so what? It had worked, and that was what was important. Now that I'd sung once with my eyes open, I was sure I could do it again.

Eyes on the prize, I thought with a secret smile, picturing myself performing a duet with Derek the way I'd just done with Nico—but with a much different ending. *Eyes on the prize!*

When I stepped into the auditorium the next afternoon for auditions, the first person I saw was Derek. Great. Nothing like a little extra pressure to turn the ol' swooping pterodactyl stomach into a herd of galloping brontosauruses. Or was it brontosauri?

"Maggie! Hi!" Derek hurried toward me, looking majestic in his flannel shirt, faded jeans, and high-top sneakers. "Whoa, I didn't think I'd be this nervous." He chuckled sheepishly. "I mean, I figured it would be sort of like regular team tryouts and stuff."

Sternly ordering myself not to faint or grab his butt or do anything else embarrassing, I smiled back. "Yeah," I said. "It's always, um, you know, scary or whatever. Auditioning, I mean. You know—for a play. Or a musical. Not, like, football. Like you were saying. Isn't that what you were saying? Um, or whatever . . ."

If he noticed I was babbling like an idiot, he didn't let it show. He was glancing around the auditorium. Dozens of people were there, bent over their scripts or sheet music, practicing with their friends, or just milling around looking anxious. In addition to the usual gang of Thespians, there were plenty of other students present. We usually got all kinds of people trying out for the plays, with at least a handful of non-Thespians getting cast.

"This is wild," Derek said. "I guess I never realized the school play was such a big deal."

I probably should have been insulted. Glenn certainly would have been if he'd been close enough to hear rather than half-way across the auditorium gesticulating wildly at the wall in preparation. But as far as I was concerned, it didn't matter what Derek said. All that mattered was that he was talking to *me*.

Just then Calla rushed past, heading for the stage. "Wish me luck, you guys!" she called to me and Derek over her shoulder. "I'm up first!"

"Break a leg!" I called to her.

Nearby, Duane stood up from his seat

as Calla took the stage. "Knock 'em dead, baby!" he hollered.

Calla blew him a kiss, then glanced down at Nico, who was seated at the piano in the orchestra pit. "Ready when you are," she said, sounding confident.

Nico started to play, and Calla started to sing. True to form, she was auditioning with the title song from *Cabaret*, as sung by the female lead, Sally Bowles. She believes in going for the gusto.

"Wow, she's good," Derek said as we watched. "I never would have guessed she could sing so well."

I wondered if his surprise had anything to do with her weight. For some reason, people tend to underestimate Calla. She claims it's because skinny people automatically think fat girls can't do anything, and I wasn't sure she was entirely wrong. It just didn't seem fair. I wanted to say that to Derek, but didn't quite have the guts.

That's probably not what he meant, anyway, I told myself. *Besides, he can see how talented she is for himself. Why make him feel bad?*

In any case, I didn't have much time to worry about it. As soon as Calla was finished, Ms. Dana called Derek's name.

"Here goes nothing." He grinned at me and loped off.

"Break a leg," I called after him.

My secret imagination doesn't only concoct good stories. Sometimes it comes up with worst-case scenarios. For instance, over the past day or two I had started imagining what might happen if it turned out Derek couldn't sing after all. What if I'd gone through all this for nothing? What if he got laughed off the stage, stormed out, and decided to take up knitting instead of theater?

But I needn't have worried. Derek handed Nico some sheet music and climbed onto the stage. He looked really comfortable there, standing with his hands in his pockets as he surveyed the auditorium with an easy smile.

Nico started to play, and as soon as Derek opened his mouth to sing, I smiled with relief. He was good—*really* good. His voice was a rich baritone, confident and pleasant.

"Not bad, not bad at all," Calla said, walking up the aisle to join me halfway through Derek's audition.

I smiled at her. "I could say the same

thing about you," I said. "Sally Bowles, here you come!"

"Are you kidding? Fat girls don't get cast as Sally Bowles." But by the way she was smiling, I couldn't quite tell if she meant it or not.

Anyway, I was kind of distracted by Derek, who was still singing. "You may be watching your leading man up there," I told Calla. "He's amazing!"

Duane wandered over to join us just in time to hear my comment. "Yeah, I gotta admit, the boy can blow," he said. "You sure know how to pick 'em, Maggie."

I shushed him as Derek finished and stepped down off the stage. He came toward us, grinning in a charmingly sheepish way.

"Okay, you guys didn't run screaming from the room, at least," he said with a laugh. "So, was that okay?"

Duane gave him a friendly punch on the arm. "More than okay," he assured him. "You're a natural!"

"Thanks." Derek slung his arm around my shoulders and gave a squeeze. "And thanks for talking to me beforehand, Maggie. Kept me from getting too nervous." Dropping his arm, he checked his watch. "Oops! Better roll—guys are waiting for me. Catch you later!"

With that, he was gone. And I melted into a puddle on the auditorium floor. Well, almost. Actually I sort of staggered over and collapsed onto the arm of the nearest seat.

"Oh," I said. "My," I went on. "God!" I finished, letting out my breath in a whoosh. "Did you guys see that? He put his arm around me!"

That was enough to keep me floating on cloud nine for the next half hour until it was my turn to audition. I was barely aware of the other auditions, though I did come out of my Derek-induced coma just long enough to notice and applaud Duane's rollicking, crowd-pleasing rendition of "If I Were a Rich Man" from *Fiddler on the Roof*.

Finally, though, Ms. Dana called my name. That snapped me out of my stupor, and I remembered why I was there. Oh, right. Singing. Gulp.

Feeling the fear building in me as I climbed onstage, I glanced frantically down at Nico in the orchestra pit. He lifted one hand from the piano keys long enough to shoot me a thumbs-up.

"Ready to go, Maggie?" Ms. Dana asked

cheerfully. She was sitting in the front row with a clipboard, watching all the auditions. "Whenever you're ready."

I wasn't ready. Then again, it seemed unlikely I'd ever be ready for this. So I just nodded at Nico, took a deep breath, and closed my eyes.

"Is the list up?" Duane called down the hall.

"What do you think, genius? I'm sure all those people are standing there staring at the wall for no reason," Calla retorted, sounding a bit breathless. The three of us had just run all the way from the student parking lot to the music wing. It was the morning after auditions, and we were all nervous.

Okay, that's a lie. *They* were nervous. *I* was practically having a meltdown, even though I was pretty sure I'd done okay on my song yesterday. After auditions were over, Nico had even come over to me to say it was the best I'd ever sounded. If he'd noticed I'd kept my eyes squeezed shut the entire time, he was nice enough not to comment on it.

But none of that would matter if I didn't get cast. What if I'd gone through all the trauma and extra practice for nothing?

In any case, I would know soon enough. It was obvious that the list was up. Most of the drama club was milling around in front of the music department bulletin board, along with a bunch of other people— though even in my anxious haze I couldn't help noticing there was no sign of Derek. There was such a crowd that even tall Duane couldn't see the list over people's heads.

"Coming through," Calla said loudly, pushing her way between Jenna Paolini and some freshman-looking kid. After one glance at the list, she let out a loud gasp. "Oh my god, Mags. You did it. You did it!"

"What?" I craned my neck, wishing I were taller. The Paolini twins' heads were bobbing around right in front of me, their wavy hair blocking my view of the list. "You mean I actually got a part?"

"No," she said, and for a moment my heart sank. Then she turned toward me, her eyes wide. "You got *the* part. Maggie, you're playing Sally Bowles. You landed the lead!"

Eight

For a second I thought she was kidding. Then the Paolini twins' hair parted like the Red Sea, finally offering me a look at the list. And there it was.

EMCEE: DUANE CLAYTON
CLIFF BRADSHAW: DEREK O'MALLEY
SALLY BOWLES: MAGGIE TANNERY

I didn't bother to read any further. My mind had gone all wobbly at the sight of my name up there. Because unless I was going crazy, Calla was right. I'd landed the lead. The only trouble was, I didn't want it!

"Is this a joke?" I blurted out, staring at the letters of my name so hard, I'm surprised

I didn't burn a hole through the paper. "I can't play Sally!"

"Obviously, Ms. Dana disagrees. Anyway, I thought you'd be happy. This is your big chance." Calla stabbed at the list with one plump finger. "Loverboy is playing Cliff, see? Romantic leads, just like Romeo and Juliet but with a lot more dancing and a lot less poison and stabbing and stuff."

"I don't care. I can't do it." My mind was still rebelling against this, frantic at the thought of playing Sally. It was one thing to close my eyes when I was just standing there singing. But we'd rented *Cabaret* the previous weekend, in addition to reading through the script, so I had a pretty good idea of what the part involved. Sally Bowles was a spunky British girl who falls in and out of love with an American writer in 1930s Berlin while making her living singing at a seedy club. And she didn't just have to sing. She had to dance, too. And despite Nico's best efforts, I'd only made it through the audition by closing my eyes. No way was I going to be able to dance with my eyes shut!

Duane and Calla exchanged a concerned look. "Look, Maggie," Duane said. "If you didn't want a big part, you shouldn't have done such a great job at the tryouts yesterday. You sounded like a pro up there. Seriously."

"Are you kidding me? I mean, sure, maybe I pulled off one song. With my eyes shut. And only a few people watching. But carrying a whole show?" I shuddered. "No, I should just go tell Ms. Dana right now. Why string everybody along? Maybe I could offer to be the understudy for Sally instead. That way I could still rehearse and everything, but I probably wouldn't have to actually perform . . ."

Before my friends could answer, Nico hurried over. "Hey, congrats," he said to me, running one hand through his spiky black hair and grinning. "I just heard the news. We did it, huh?"

"This is a disaster!" I blurted out, grabbing him by the arm. I think I even shook him a little. "I can't do this!"

"Huh?" Nico's smile faded, and he looked perplexed as he yanked his arm away. "What are you talking about? I thought you'd be happy."

"Well, I'm not." I glared at him as if this was all his fault. Actually, in a way it sort of was. "At least, not unless you can teach me to dance with my eyes shut!"

He lifted one hand as if to touch my arm, then dropped it again. "Look, don't panic, okay?" he said. "You sang with your eyes open once, remember? You can do it again if you work on it. I'll keep helping you if you want."

"Hear that?" Calla said. "Listen to Nico. He got you this far, right? If he thinks you can do this, and Ms. Dana thinks you can do this, and we think you can do this . . ." She gestured to herself and Duane. "Well, who are you to argue?"

A new voice broke in before I could answer. "Hey, leading lady!"

I looked over my shoulder to see Derek loping toward us with a big smile on his face. The door at the end of the hallway behind him was propped open, and the morning light pouring through sort of made it look like a halo was surrounding his entire body. He looked more gorgeous than ever, and it made my mind stall out for a second.

"Congrats, Derek," Calla said, as cool as ever. "Or should I say Cliff?"

He grinned in an adorable aw-shucks kind of way. "Thanks. Beginner's luck, I guess. Actually, I'm kind of nervous—I wasn't expecting to get such a big part."

"You'll do fine," Duane said. "Maggie will be up there helping you the whole time. Right, Maggie?"

I glared at him. Yeah, I'd be sure to thank him for that later. Now, how was I supposed to break the news to Derek—the leading man of my dreams—that I couldn't go through with this?

"Actually, I was going to ask you about that." Derek turned toward me. "Ms. Dana told me the first read-through will be Friday morning. If you have time, do you maybe want to get together tomorrow after school and read through our parts? We could grab one of those back booths at the Dairy Queen. I'll buy you a milk shake or something." He shrugged. "I mean, I know this is probably no big deal to a real actor like you, but I can use all the help I can get. It would be great to prep a little before I have to do it in front of everyone, you know?"

I just gaped at him for a second. Once again, I had the strange feeling that my fantasies were escaping into reality. Derek O'Malley wanted me to run lines with him? In a private booth at Dairy Queen? Buying me a milk shake? Was it my imagination, or did that sound almost like . . . a *date*?

"Um . . . okay," I managed to blurt out. "Sounds like a plan."

"Great!" He looked relieved. "Meet you in the parking lot after school tomorrow. Thanks, Maggie!"

"Yeah. Um, I mean, okay. I mean, you're welcome. See you then," I spit out the words with some effort. By then, he was halfway down the hall.

"So does this mean you're going to accept the part?" Calla demanded as soon as he was gone.

She stared at me. So did Duane. Nico kind of glared out of the corner of his eye in his usual I'm-too-cool-to-care way.

I glanced down the hall at Derek's retreating back. His tall, strong, handsome, muscular back. The back that would be sitting across from me in a booth at the Dairy Queen in approximately thirty-one hours—not that I was counting.

"Hey, what can I say?" I said grimly, trying not to think too hard about what I was getting myself into. "Life is a cabaret."

It wasn't until a few minutes later, after I calmed down a little, that I realized I hadn't even noticed whether Calla had been cast. By now the crowd had thinned out as most people—including Duane and Nico—had hurried off to their lockers or club meetings or homerooms. Calla and I were sitting on the bench in the music suite hallway. She was listening to me babble senselessly about Derek while we both waited for my legs to stop shaking enough for me to walk to homeroom. So I had a clear view as we stood up and stepped closer to the bulletin board.

"Hey," I said as I scanned the list. "You're playing Fraulein Schneider. That's a pretty big part!"

"Well, I'm a pretty big actress, so that works." Calla chuckled, doing a quick version of her boom-boom move. "But yeah, I'm psyched. Too bad Duane blew it—I was hoping he'd get to play Herr Schultz."

I grinned, knowing she was (at least mostly) kidding. Sure, it would be nice for the two of them to play a couple again. But the Emcee was probably the most important role in the whole play, and Duane was perfect for it. I was also impressed that Calla had held in her glee at her own success for so long while listening to me whine. That was a good friend for you.

"Yeah, lucky you," I added after another glance at the list. "Looks like you'll get to test your acting skills to the limit by pretending to be in love with Glenn."

Calla grimaced slightly, then shrugged. "If you could do it, I can do it too," she says. "It shall be my biggest acting challenge ever." She smirked. "Unlike *your* leading man, huh? You won't need to do much acting there."

I shivered. Now that my initial panic attack at playing Sally had started to wear off, it was being replaced by the nearly unfathomable concept that my dreams were coming true. I was going to be Derek O'Malley's leading lady.

The thought was terrifying.

I'd thought I was nervous before auditions. But that was nothing compared to how I felt walking out of my last class the following afternoon. I hadn't really talked to Derek since he'd asked me to run lines. Well, except for a couple of times when he passed me in the hall and said hi, and I responded with my usual "urgle gurgle glug" type of response.

Hurrying to my locker, I dumped all

my books on the bottom shelf and then scrambled for my makeup kit and hairbrush. I brushed out my hair first, slicked on my favorite raspberry-flavored tinted lip gloss, then dabbed on a touch of blush for good measure. Was it too much? I wanted to look my best, but not as if I was trying too hard. How embarrassing would it be if Derek guessed I'd tarted myself up for our "date"? I was pooching my lips at myself in the little mirror inside the locker door, trying to decide whether to remove the blush, when I heard someone clear his throat behind me.

I whirled around, almost slamming the locker door shut on my own hand. Nico was standing there.

"Oh!" I exclaimed. "You scared me half to death."

"Sorry." He stared at me. Was he wondering why I had on so much makeup? Or was that just my paranoid imagination? "Listen, my band practice got canceled," he said. "Want to hang out and start working on your songs this afternoon?"

"No!" I blurted out. The only thought more terrifying than my meeting with Derek was the thought of anything *delaying* my meeting with Derek. Hey, nobody ever said true love was logical! "Um, I mean, thanks. That would be cool and all. But I can't today."

"Oh. Okay." Nico shrugged. "See you."

"Bye," I said. At least I think I did. I was so nervous that my mind seemed to be shutting down. All I could hear as I turned and walked down the hall was a sort of loud ringing sound in my ears.

Well, until Calla caught up to me. "Ready for your big date, sweetie?" she bellowed cheerfully into my ear. Or maybe it just seemed like a bellow to me. I grabbed her, shushing her wildly. I probably sounded like a vacuum cleaner.

"What if he hears you?" I hissed, my eyes darting back and forth as I scanned the halls for any sign of Derek. "He probably doesn't think this is, um, you know." I lowered my voice to the barest whisper. "A date."

"Whatever." Calla rolled her eyes. "Glad to see you're handling this so well."

I glared at her. "Some friend you are," I said. "Look, can you walk me out to the parking lot? You know—for moral support."

"Sure, sweetie. Let's go."

The walk out to the parking lot takes less than five minutes, but on that particular day it seemed more like five years. Calla did her best to distract me on the way by telling a funny story about how Duane had pretended to swallow a test tube in their chemistry class. But that only helped a little.

When we got out there, there was no sign of Derek. My heart sank into the toes of my shoes. What if I'd misunderstood him? What if there was actually no "date" at all? What if he'd had a better offer and forgotten all about our plans? I could see the tragic stage version now:

GRIZZLED POLICE OFFICER, *through bull-horn*: Maggie Tannery! Get down from that bell tower before someone gets hurt.

ME, *waving automatic rifle*: No! I can't take it anymore!

GPO: All right, don't panic, Miss Tannery. There's someone here we think you might want to talk to.

DEREK, *stepping into view with a bikini-clad cheerleader on each arm*: Yo, um, what's her name again?

GPO, *whispering*: It's Maggie.

DEREK: Oh, right! Margie, I mean Maggie. Whazzup?

ME, *insanely*: Derek, my love! Why did you stand me up for our date?

DEREK: Date? Oh, you mean reading lines? You thought that was a date?

[DEREK laughs. CHEERLEADERS giggle. Even GPO hides a disdainful smile.]

ME, *sobbing and raising rifle*: I knew it! Good-bye, cruel world . . .

GPO: Maggie, no!

"Maggie? Yo!" Calla poked me in the arm. Hard.

"Ow!" I cried, snapping out of my sick little fantasy world. Rubbing my arm, I glared at her. "Look, this is stupid. He probably forgot. Or got a better offer. Or—"

"Shut up, please." Calla waggled her eyebrows meaningfully, then nodded toward something over my shoulder. "Here he comes."

I gasped and spun around. Sure enough, Derek was walking toward us. He lifted one hand and smiled. "Sorry I'm late!" he called, breaking into a jog.

"See you," Calla whispered to me. For a big girl, she can disappear awfully fast.

The next few minutes were a blur. Seriously. I sort of remembered getting into Derek's car and thinking, *OMG, I'm in Derek's car!* Then there was more blur, and then I was thinking, *OMG, I'm walking into DQ with Derek!* and then a few minutes later, *OMG, Derek is sitting right across from me! He's looking at me! Why is he staring at me like that?*

I guess that was when it dawned on me that I was going to have to start acting a lot more sane. And soon. That probably meant speaking in actual human words of more than one syllable.

"So," he said, "want a soda or something?"

"Um, no," I replied. "Thanks. Not thirsty." I didn't bother to mention that if I tried to drink anything at that moment, I'd probably wind up choking on it and spitting it all over him. Somehow, it didn't seem like a selling point.

"Okay. Guess we should get started, then." He pulled out a copy of the script. Flipping through it, he set it on the table between us, angled so we could both read from it. "I thought maybe we could just start with the scene in the Kit Kat Klub where Cliff and Sally first meet, and go from there."

"Sounds . . . ," I started. "Um, sounds . . ."

Good! Sounds good! my mind shrieked at me. Somehow, though, my mouth refused to pick up the hint. To cover up my consternation, I raised my hand and coughed.

"You okay?" Derek looked concerned.

"Fine," I choked out. "Go ahead. Let's read."

I was hoping I would relax a little once we got started. After all, that had worked supremely well the last time we'd acted together.

But this time, not so much. Derek read his first line; I think it was something complicated like "Hello." After that, Sally was supposed to ask him if he was English. Easy, right?

Not exactly. "You . . . I . . . ," I stammered, staring helplessly from the script in front of me to his dazzling face. At that moment, I knew that this wasn't going to work. It wasn't going to be a repeat of our *Romeo and Juliet* magic. I just wasn't prepared to be here right now, with him, my dream come true. It was like stepping onstage to perform the lead in a show you'd never rehearsed.

He was staring at me again. I had to do something. Otherwise it was only a matter of time before I became known around school as "that weird Tannery chick."

"Sorry," I blurted out, sliding over so fast on the smooth plastic seat that I almost shot off the end of the booth and fell on my butt. I saved myself just in time by grabbing the edge of the table. "I'm sorry. I—I can't do this."

"What?" He looked surprised and disappointed, though I couldn't imagine why. It couldn't be that appealing to be stuck in a small booth with a total blithering psycho.

I grabbed my neck. "Sore throat," I said, putting a bit of a rasp in my voice. "Thought it was getting better. But now it feels worse again. I should go home and take a nap."

"Oh, bummer. Well, maybe another time. Want me to drive you home?" Derek was already making like he was going to stand up.

"No thanks. I live close." That wasn't really true. But I figured a nice two-mile jog might do me some good right about then.

"Okay. Feel better."

"Thanks." I didn't dare meet his eye as I turned and fled.

Nine

"And then what did you do?" Calla asked, sounding perplexed.

"I told you! I ran out of the DQ like a total nut job," I said with a frown. "I just needed to get away and clear my head. Being there alone with him freaked me out." I took a deep breath. "But I'm okay now. Next time I'll be ready."

"Okay." She sounded dubious.

It was Friday morning, and I'd just spent our short drive to school giving Calla a hurried report on yesterday's disastrous nondate. She'd been off visiting her grandparents by the time I got home, so I hadn't had a chance to tell her sooner.

Now we were walking down the hall,

heading for Mr. Fayne's classroom. We all still called it that, even though Mr. Fayne wasn't coming back. None of us seemed ready to start calling it "Ms. Dana's room" or "the Thespian room" or its actual official name, "Room 9-E." To us it had always been Mr. Fayne's room, and that was how we would always think of it.

It was time for the first read-through. We weren't starting official after-school rehearsals in the auditorium until Monday, but Ms. Dana thought it was a good idea for us to get together and read through the script before the weekend. Something about allowing us to start living with our characters, or something like that.

"I'm serious," I told Calla, taking a long, cleansing breath. "I thought about it all last night, and I decided it's just like that first time I tried out for the play. I need to stop overthinking and go with the flow, and I'll be fine."

"Okay," Calla said again. "I hope you're right, sweetie. Because I don't like seeing you so freaked out all the time. It's not healthy."

We'd reached the room by then, so there was no more time for discussion, though I strongly suspected I hadn't heard the last of this. Calla isn't the type of person to hold back her opinions.

Inside, most of the cast was already seated. Even Nico was there, fiddling with what looked like some kind of recording device. Ms. Dana was perched on the edge of the desk as usual, her short legs swinging.

"Come on in, Sally, Fraulein Schneider," she called out when she saw us, beaming with her usual giddy cheer. "Or should I say *Willkommen*? We're almost all here." She checked her watch. "Derek said he might be a little late, but we can get started without him on the opening scene with the Emcee and the Kit Kat Girls. You guys don't need to sing yet—just read out your lyrics and start thinking about what they mean. Internalize them, allow them to sink into your psyche, and let them blossom back out as your own. Ready, Duane?"

"Ready as I'll ever be." Duane grinned and lifted his script. He started reading off his opening song as I sat down in an empty seat and pulled out my own copy of the script.

While Duane and the Kit Kat Girls were doing their thing, I flipped through the script until I found the beginning of my part. In between my bouts of self-recrimination the previous night, I'd started studying my lines. At least that was something I knew how to do, unlike almost everything else about this role. . . .

"Sorry I'm late!"

My head snapped up so fast, I'm surprised I didn't end up with whiplash. Derek had just come into the room.

"Just in time, buddy," Duane said. "You're up in, like, three lines."

"It's all right, Derek," Ms. Dana said. "Have a seat, and just pick up the reading as soon as you're ready."

Derek glanced around and caught me staring at him. He grinned and hurried over, sliding into the empty desk right next to mine.

"Whew!" he murmured to me, leaning closer. "Glad I didn't get yelled at for being late on the first day."

I just smiled in return, unable to speak. I'd thought I was prepared to face him again. I'd thought wrong. He was so close that I could smell some musky, sweet, mysterious scent wafting off him. I assumed it was his aftershave. I also assumed it wasn't actually concocted of opium and other mind-altering substances, though you couldn't tell it from the way my mind and body were reacting. If my life had been a cartoon, I would already be drifting up out of my chair, my nose leading the way as I floated through the air following the scent waves emanating from him. As it was, I just sat there breathing it in and feeling sort of giddy and confused.

Luckily my part didn't start for a few more pages. While Derek traded lines with Tommy and some sophomore kid, who were playing Ernst Ludwig and a German customs officer, respectively, I took deep breaths and tried to focus. After all, I wasn't nervous, shy, easily distracted Maggie Tannery right now. I was Sally Bowles—self-confident, free-spirited, ready to go after the life and the man I wanted. Closing my eyes, I tried to become Sally—charming Sally, talented Sally . . .

"Sally," Ms. Dana broke into my reverie some time later. "Sally! Are you with us, Maggie?"

Derek leaned across the aisle and poked me in the arm. "You're up, Maggie," he said.

"Oh!" I sat up straight, flustered as I realized they'd reached my entrance while

I was spacing out trying to get into character. Apparently I'd totally missed Calla's first scene with Glenn, among other things. "Um, sorry." The spot on my arm where Derek had touched me was tingling, which was a little distracting. Scanning my script, I searched for my first line. "Um . . ."

"It's okay, Maggie," Ms. Dana said soothingly. "Let's back up—take it from the Emcee's intro, okay?"

Duane nodded and launched into his introduction of Sally Bowles for her first number at the Kit Kat Klub. I swallowed hard, imagining how nerve-wracking it was going to be to step out onstage and *sing* my first line. What had I gotten myself into, anyway?

I glanced over at Derek, trying to remind myself exactly why I was doing this. He shot me an encouraging smile, which made me forget everything else for a moment. The result?

"Maggie?" Ms. Dana said. "That's your cue—the Emcee says your name, and then you start your first song."

She was looking at me sort of strangely. And no wonder. Everyone had probably told her I was some great actress, and here I was acting like I'd never even seen a script before. Talk about embarrassing!

"Sorry!" I gasped out. "I've got it . . ."

"She has a sore throat," Derek spoke up helpfully. He turned and smiled at me again. "Is that still bothering you, Maggie?"

"No," I blurted out, then immediately regretted it. Stupid, stupid me! Why hadn't I taken his cue? Acting so weird because of a sore throat might make me look like a prima donna or a hypochondriac. But that had to be better than looking like an incompetent loser, didn't it? "Um, I'm okay. I've got it."

I glanced down at my script. The words of the song swam on the page, refusing to hold still long enough for me to read them. Luckily, I'd memorized most of the song the night before. I managed to get out the first two or three lines before stumbling over the word "inkling." It kept coming out as "inking" instead.

"Inking," I said for the second or third time. "Oops! Um, I mean inking. Linking! No, *inking*. Ling."

"Hang on." Ms. Dana slid off the desk and stood up. "Maybe we're getting ahead of ourselves here. After all, we hardly know one another, right? This must be a big emotional stretch for all of you, having me come in and take over for Mr. Fayne so abruptly."

"Sort of, I guess," Duane said for all of us.

Ms. Dana nodded. "I'm thinking this read-through can wait," she said. "I mean, I'm sure you've all read the script by now, right?" She glanced around, apparently satisfied with the number of nods she saw in response to her question. "Good. Then let's try a little improv exercise."

Uh-oh. That sounded kind of ominous. Mr. Fayne had never been the type of director who believed in improv exercises. He always said you learned to act by acting, not by pretending to be a chicken or a blade of grass or whatever.

"Everyone come up here to the front where we have some space," Ms. Dana ordered happily. "Then close your eyes and just start *moving* like you think your character would move when nobody is looking. Don't think about it, just *feel* it. Be free to do whatever comes to you."

Nobody reacted at first. I think we were all kind of confused.

"Um, we don't really have to do that," Lizzy Paolini spoke up at last. "I mean,

III

Maggie probably just isn't much of a morning person. I'm sure she'll wake up soon and remember how to read."

I shot her a glance. Thanks, Lizzy. Way to make me sound like even more of a doofus.

"No, I think this is a fantastic idea." Ms. Dana clapped her hands like a little kid at the circus. "It will give us all a chance to get to know ourselves and our characters better. I should have thought of it in the first place, really."

It was obvious she wasn't going to change her mind. A few people shot me annoyed glances as they got up, clearly blaming my spazzitude for having to do this.

"So do you guys do stuff like this all the time?" Derek asked me as we both stood and moved toward the front of the room.

I shook my head. "No," I choked out. "First time."

For a few moments we all just sort of stood around up there giggling awkwardly. "Close your eyes!" Ms. Dana urged, seemingly unaware of our discomfiture.

Naturally, Nico assumed he was exempt from the exercise. He was still perched on a desk with the recording thingy beside him.

Suddenly he got up and stepped toward me.

"Go on, Maggie," he said, a slightly evil glint in his eye. "You should be good at this. You already know how to do stuff with your eyes closed."

I shot him a glance. For a second I thought he was being mean. Then I realized the truth. He was teasing me. Like a friend. I hadn't known he had it in him. The thought even distracted me from feeling self-conscious in front of Derek. At least for a millisecond or two.

Finally Duane let out a shrug. "All right, I guess I might as well give this a try," he said. "Here I go . . ."

He closed his eyes and just stood there for a moment. Everyone, including me, watched him. First he started wriggling his shoulders. Then his hands got involved. He sort of clenched and unclenched them at first, which soon turned into a sinuous, snakelike movement. After that his whole body seemed to loosen up and lose all its bones, as he swayed and shimmied in place.

"Excellent!" Ms. Dana exclaimed, clapping wildly. "That's wonderful, Duane. Are you feeling your character?"

"I am!" Duane grinned, his eyes still squeezed shut. He lifted both hands and with them started to make the outline of a human body. Before long that human started looking curvier and curvier. "Oops!" he cried. "Now I think I'm feeling Calla's, er, character!"

"Why, I never!" Calla stepped over and slapped him lightly across the face. Everyone laughed, and some of the girls applauded.

"All right." Ms. Dana smiled and shook her head. "Anyway, now that Duane has showed you all what I have in mind . . ."

Duane's silliness seemed to have broken through everyone's embarrassment. Well, almost everyone. Nico had sat back down. As for me, while the others all closed their eyes and started swaying or dancing or doing jumping jacks or whatever, I just stood there, one eye open and one shut, and watched them.

"Go on, Maggie." Ms. Dana smiled at me encouragingly. "Feel your role. Become Sally."

I closed the other eye. Nico was right— I should have been used to walking around blind by then. But somehow this was much harder. To my left, I could hear Tommy stomping around like a German soldier or something. Somewhere beyond him, Calla seemed to be humming under her breath as she did her thing. And I was pretty sure Rosalie was still just off to my left waving her arms around, probably within seconds of giving me a concussion.

Doing my best to ignore all that, I tried to imagine how Sally Bowles would move when nobody was looking. But I could only concentrate on that for a few seconds before I opened my eyes, wanting to make sure nobody was peeking at me. Nobody was except for Ms. Dana and Nico, who was still watching us all with a look of detached amusement. A quick glance confirmed that Derek's eyes were shut tight. He was sort of walking around aimlessly in a small circle. Apparently he'd decided that Cliff liked to spin around like a dog getting ready for a nap.

Seeing that Ms. Dana was looking straight at me, I took a deep breath and shut my eyes before she could scold me again. Okay, I was Sally. So what would Sally do now?

I heard someone getting closer off to my left. Once again my eyes popped open of their own accord.

"Maggie!" Ms. Dana chided from her spot on the desk. What, had she been staring at me the whole time just waiting for me to crack?

"Sorry," I said. "I can't help it. My eyes just keep opening by themselves."

"Oh, I see." For a second I dared to hope she might give up and let us quit. Instead she stepped around the desk and grabbed a long, filmy red scarf that was hanging over the back of her chair. "Here, let's try this."

A few of the others opened their eyes to see what was happening. My face flamed as I realized what she had in mind. Before I could protest, I was blindfolded with her scarf. It reeked of lavender and patchouli.

"All right, there you go." Ms. Dana sounded satisfied. "Try again, my starling."

I gritted my teeth, wishing I had Calla's guts and mouth. If I did, I'd tell Ms. Dana exactly what I thought of her ridiculous improv exercise. *And* her stinky scarf.

But I wasn't Calla. So I just stood there for a moment feeling stupid. Finally I decided I might as well give this a try. What did I have to lose? Nobody but Ms. Dana and Nico could see me. Nico had already seen enough of me at my worst that I wasn't too worried about what he would think. And Ms. Dana was so weird that she'd probably think I was a genius if I started flapping my arms and doing the chicken dance.

So once again, I did my best to channel Sally Bowles. And this time it worked. A jazzy tune started playing in my head, like something one might have heard at the Kit Kat Klub. My hips started swaying, and the beat filled me. Soon I was dancing in place. It wasn't so bad. It was actually sort of freeing. I started moving more, letting the wild abandon of a fun-loving girl in prewar Berlin fill me. It was like one of my secret fantasies, and I actually started to enjoy it a little . . . at least, until I twirled a little too vigorously and crashed into someone.

"Hey!" I heard Calla exclaim.

"Sorry!" I gasped out, popping back into my own persona instantly and backing away—right into the edge of Mr. Fayne's desk. I jumped away from that, my arms outstretched blindly, and skidded on a script or something that someone had left on the floor.

"Look out!" someone cried. Nico? I wasn't sure and didn't have time to worry about it. Because I'd just caught myself by crashing into someone else. Hard.

"Oof!" was all I heard before the person I'd hit gave way and I felt myself falling, falling . . .

"Are you two all right?" Ms. Dana cried.

My elbow hurt where it had hit something—probably the edge of the desk—on the way down. Otherwise I was fine, probably because I'd broken my fall by landing directly on top of someone. I reached up and yanked off my blindfold.

"Are you okay, Maggie?" Derek asked from beneath me.

I goggled at him, not willing to believe this. Derek. I'd landed on Derek! I was straddling his chest like some cheap floozy.

"Oh!" I cried, pushing away from him. Unfortunately I pushed right on his Adam's apple. He gargled alarmingly for a second while I rolled to one side, trying desperately to disentangle myself from him.

Finally I managed to scramble to my feet. He sat up and rubbed his throat. "Whoa," he said, his voice sounding a bit hoarse. "Pretty intense acting exercise, Ms. D. I'm all choked up."

A few people laughed while Nico stepped over and offered a hand to help Derek up. "You okay, man?" he asked with concern.

"Looked like she set you down pretty hard."

By now, naturally, the rest of the group had opened their eyes. "What happened?" someone asked.

Nico seemed happy to explain. Since when had he become so chatty? Meanwhile I found myself wondering exactly what was involved in joining the Witness Protection Program. It took every ounce of self-control I had not to run screaming from the room and never come back.

"Never mind," Derek said with a laugh, brushing himself off. "Hey, at least she didn't land on my bad knee."

Yeah, I thought as everyone laughed and my face flamed. At least there was that.

Ten

I'd made arrangements to practice my singing with Nico after school that day. By the time I headed for the music suite after last period, I'd mostly recovered from that morning's humiliation. It helped that I hadn't seen Derek all day except from a distance. With any luck, the fall had given him a concussion and he wouldn't remember it was me who'd fallen on him.

Nico was already in the empty music room when I walked in. "Hi," he said. "I had a great idea. Today instead of singing, I want you to inhabit the spirit of your song by pretending you're an eggplant with dandruff."

I grimaced. He had Ms. Dana's breathy voice and inflection down pat. "Very funny,"

I said, tossing my bag onto a chair. "Can you believe what a whack job she is? I miss Mr. Fayne."

"Yeah." Nico shrugged. "Still, I guess it's good that she's shaking the Thespians out of their rut."

That was easy for him to say. He wasn't the one who'd had to learn to sing in a week and a half. But I decided not to point that out. I didn't want to alienate him when he was the only one who might be able to help me through this.

"So what should we *really* do today?" I asked.

He sat down at the piano and riffled through the sheet music on the stand. "I thought maybe we should start by working on your big final song—'Cabaret,'" he said. "If you can nail the right tone and everything on that one, the rest should be easy."

"Are you sure? I thought maybe we could work on 'Perfectly Marvelous' first."

I was kind of worried about that one. It started off as all me, but ended as a duet with Derek. I definitely wanted to be as prepared as possible for that. Otherwise I'd probably freeze up again. And after the way I'd literally thrown myself at him that morning, I didn't want to give Derek any further proof that I was a nut.

Nico was shaking his head as he pulled out the piece of music he wanted. "Nah, that one's no big deal," he said. "Once you've got the lyrics down, it should be a piece of cake vocally."

"Easy for you to say," I blurted out before I could stop myself.

He glanced over his shoulder at me. "Huh?"

Oops. I bit my lip. He looked a little annoyed. Go figure—as if I didn't have enough emotional quirks of my own, I had to get my singing lessons from the touchy musical genius. Still, like I said, I didn't want to run Nico off just when I needed him most.

"Sorry, I didn't mean that the way it sounded." I twisted my hands together and took a step toward him. "It's just, um, I'm a little worried about, you know, singing with someone. Er, Derek, specifically. He makes me, you know, kind of nervous. Not in a bad way!" I added quickly, not wanting him to think I couldn't stand Derek or something. Yeah, all I needed was for *that* little rumor to get back to him! "In a good way, actually." I smiled, feeling myself blushing as I recalled that *Romeo and Juliet* scene. Sometimes I thought that memory was the only thing keeping me going. "In a really good way," I added softly, speaking more to myself now than to Nico.

"Oh." Nico's left eyebrow twitched slightly, but the rest of his face remained impassive. "I see."

He turned around to face the piano again and tossed off a few quick scales. I waited for a second, doing some of the breathing exercises and little facial massage moves he'd taught me.

"Um, so are we doing 'Perfectly Marvelous'?" I asked hesitantly after listening to a few more scales.

"If that's what you want, that's what you'll get," he said without turning.

He sounded annoyed again. But I tried not to worry about it. He would get over it. At least I hoped so. My relationship with Derek—the real-life one, not the fantasy-world one—depended on it.

The following Monday was our first "real" rehearsal. We all gathered in the auditorium after the final bell. Ms. Dana was waiting for us there, standing in the middle of the empty stage. I sneaked a peek at Derek as I took a seat in the first row between Calla and Rosalie. He was standing in the open area between the seats and the orchestra pit, one foot propped on the arm of an empty chair, leaning over and chatting with Nico, who had just sat down in the second row.

"Welcome, Thespians!" Ms. Dana cried, spreading her arms like a preacher in the pulpit. "I hope you're all looking forward to this grand adventure as much as I am."

A few people cheered. Others sort of mumbled and shrugged. I glanced over at Calla and rolled my eyes. She grinned at me in return.

"We're ready, Ms. Dana," Duane called out. He was sitting on Calla's other side, but now he jumped to his feet and pumped both fists in the air. "Let's rock and roll!"

She smiled. "I appreciate your enthusiasm, Duane," she said. Clasping her hands together, she surveyed the rest of us. "Now, since we still haven't done a full read-through, I suppose we should begin with that today."

I heaved a silent sigh of relief. After Friday morning's disaster, I'd feared we were in for a full semester's worth of crazy improv exercises. I reached into my bag, which was sitting at my feet, and started fishing around for my script.

But, as it turned out, my relief was premature. "But here's how we're going to make it interesting," Ms. Dana went on. "Instead of just sitting around reading, I want you to get up onstage. Don't worry about blocking or anything just yet. Try to think back to our movement experiment from the other day, and build on that."

"You want us to do the read-through with our eyes closed?" Bethany, who was playing Fraulein Kost, called out. "How are we supposed to read our scripts that way?"

"Yeah. I haven't memorized my part yet." Freshman Gary Kellaway looked anxious. He was playing a waiter and only had one shared song and a single additional line. But it was his first time with any lines at all, and I understood how he felt. I'd been there, and not so long ago.

"Plus I'll probably fall off the stage," Duane put in.

"Yeah," Calla agreed. "He will."

Ms. Dana chuckled. "Don't worry, you don't have to close your eyes this time," she said. "I just want you to feel free to move around while you read, that's all. Feel the words. Let it all flow—movement, text, feeling . . ."

Before long we were all up onstage wandering around. Duane came to the front and started us off by reading out his opening song again. Ms. Dana had already explained that we weren't going to try to put any of the show to music just yet.

"After another rehearsal or two, Mr. Vasquez will start accompanying us, and you can begin singing your parts as you become comfortable with that," she'd said, sweeping one arm at Nico, who was still slouched in the second row with his boots propped up on the seat in front of him. "And of course the dancing will come a bit later still. For now, we shall focus on the words, for words are the backbone of the theater, the lifeblood in the body of our play."

After Duane and the Kit Kat Girls went through the first scene, Derek took over, reading out the lines for the scene when Cliff first arrives in Berlin by train. While he was talking to the other characters, he did a little choo-choo move with his arm.

I'm pretty sure he did it as a joke, but Ms. Dana seemed delighted.

Then it was time for Calla's entrance. Her character, Fraulein Schneider, was an older German woman who ran the boardinghouse where Cliff lived. She traded lines with Derek and a few others, and also recited her first song. I smiled as I watched her. She already had the world-weary-yet-hopeful tone of the character down pat.

Partway through the scene, the others were joined by Herr Schultz, an older Jewish shopkeeper who also lived in the boardinghouse and was in love with Fraulein Schneider. Glenn stepped forward, clearing his throat and reading out his lines with all the seriousness of Laurence Olivier playing Hamlet.

After that I kind of stopped paying attention. My part was coming up soon, and I wanted to make sure there wasn't a repeat of last week's humiliating disaster. Flipping forward, I checked out the first couple of lines of my first song, "Don't Tell Mama," which I would be performing with backup from the Kit Kat Girls.

Glancing out at the almost-empty auditorium, I realized that in less than two short months I was supposed to be singing the song onstage in front of a packed house. The idea gave me palpitations. As I was about to start hyperventilating right there on the stage, my gaze landed on Nico. Seeing him there made me relax, at least a little. Nico had brought me this far. He'd get me through this. I just had to focus on that and not freak out.

The upside of my moment of panic was that I more or less forgot to be self-conscious in front of Derek. So when my cue came, I was able to read off my lines like a normal person. Yes, even the word "inkling." Whew!

But then came the scene directly after the song, when Sally and Cliff first meet. Could I pull it off? Would it be a repeat of the magic of *Romeo and Juliet*? Or would I be reduced to a preverbal state again as soon as I looked at Derek?

A miracle. I managed to stay in character, my ability to immerse myself in my part came through for me, and Sally/I bantered with Cliff/Derek like an old pro. I even started to feel a little of that connection come back. The way he looked at me. His smile. The feeling between us . . .

But soon I would face my biggest challenge yet. The scene we were reading was supposed to take place on New Year's Eve, 1930. As the clock struck midnight, the script called for Cliff to impulsively kiss Sally.

Oh. My. God, I thought as the moment got closer. Shooting Calla a panicked look, I "accidentally" wandered a few yards away from Derek just before the kissing part and did a little shimmy-type movement, hoping Ms. Dana would think I was just "feeling my character" or whatever. In the meantime, Derek read out his "Happy New Year" line, and the moment passed without comment—or kiss. Whew. I guessed that the kiss was considered part of the blocking we weren't supposed to worry about yet.

Not that I was opposed to kissing Derek, you understand. After all, I'd done that (and maybe more) hundreds of times in my imagination. But this was different. This was real life. Why did that make it so much harder?

I tried not to worry about it for now, and soon relaxed back into Sally. At one point she—er, I—even reached over and touched Cliff—er, Derek—lightly on one arm. What can I say without sounding like Ms. Dana? It just felt right. My fingers tingled, and we smiled at each other.

Then Derek had to look down at his script for his next line. Ms. Dana took the opportunity to break in, clapping her hands.

"Nice work, Maggie!" she called. "Don't be afraid to touch him again if you feel like it. Grab him and kiss him if you feel like it!"

"Whoa, now I feel like a piece of meat!" Derek joked as several other people laughed.

Meanwhile I could feel Sally slipping away, and awkward, anxious Maggie returning as Ms. Dana continued. "You'll have to limit your kissing and touching to the proper moments later on, of course. But in these early rehearsals, it's more important to get in touch with your character and do whatever it takes to reach full understanding. Remember, you're supposed to be terribly attracted to Cliff, so go ahead and show it!"

That was all it took to turn me into a blithering idiot. I flubbed my next couple of lines, stumbling over every other word. Luckily the scene was almost over, and I was able to step back and allow others to take over for a few minutes.

I hardly dared to glance over at Derek to see what he thought of my latest display of idiocy. To my relief, he wasn't even looking at me. He was flipping through his script, probably looking for his next set of lines.

Closing my eyes, I held back a melancholy sigh. Now that rehearsals had started, it was really sinking in—things were going to be a lot different than they were in the old days with Mr. Fayne. And I'd never dealt too well with change.

I opened my eyes again just in time to catch Derek glancing over at me. When he caught my eye, he rolled his own eyes toward Ms. Dana, who was currently urging Glenn to "release your inner shopkeeper!" and made a crazy-person face. I giggled. He grinned, winked, then turned back to his script.

My heart thumped and I smiled to myself. Okay. Maybe sometimes change could be good.

Eleven

"Are you going to finish that?" Calla stared at the leftover grapes on my lunch tray.

"All yours." I pushed the tray toward her. It was Wednesday, and we were sitting at one end of an otherwise deserted table in the big, skylighted Thornton High School cafeteria. Lunch period was almost over. Duane had skipped lunch to make up a history test, and Tommy and Rosalie had already run off to a yearbook committee meeting, leaving just the two of us in our usual seats.

"Thanks." Calla grabbed a grape and popped it into her mouth. "So I wonder what theater-of-the-absurd torture Ms. Dana has in store for us this afternoon."

I grimaced. After the relatively normal read-through on Monday, Ms. Dana had been up to her old tricks again the following day. As soon as we'd walked into rehearsal, she'd announced that we would all have to lie on our backs on the stage and read through the play again. Something about "acting with our voices." It was pretty weird, though at least it meant I hadn't had to worry about the touchy-feely stuff with Derek.

"Who knows?" I said. "I'm just hoping she doesn't make us act with our underwear on outside our clothes or something. You know, like, to represent the way the world was turned inside out by the rise of the Third Reich."

Calla was still laughing at that one when Gary Kellaway rushed up to our table. Gary belonged to every extracurricular the school offered, from student council to chess club, and threw himself into each of them with equally over-the-top enthusiasm.

"Hi, you guys! Great rehearsal yesterday, huh?" Gary was clutching a digital camera. "Listen, Maggie. I want to propose a feature story for the school paper about the musical, and it would be great if I had some fun photos of our leading lady to show at our next meeting. What do you say?" He shot me a hopeful, gap-toothed smile and held up his camera.

One of Gary's many extracurriculars is our high school newspaper, the *Thornton Reporter*. From what I hear, the *Reporter* is actually pretty good as high school papers go. It's very competitive, and everyone who writes for it is always scrambling for bylines. It was no wonder Gary was looking for something to set himself apart from the crowd.

"Sure," I said. "I guess so. Um, what do you want me to do?"

"Great! Thanks, Maggie. Hang on, let me get Derek . . ." Gary turned and started waving frantically across the half-empty cafeteria.

Meanwhile I gulped and shot Calla a glance. Derek was involved in this? Suddenly a simple snapshot didn't sound so simple anymore.

But it was too late to back out now. Derek was already loping toward us, half-eaten apple in one hand.

"Ready, dude?" he asked Gary with a friendly punch on the arm. He took one more bite of his apple, then tossed the rest into the nearest trash can. "Let's do this thing."

"Great." Gary fiddled with the settings on his camera. "The light's actually pretty good in here. How about if you two pose right there by the wall."

Derek nodded and stepped over. Then he glanced at me, clearly expecting me to join him.

"Go on," Calla hissed. She gave me a hard poke in the side, which made me jump and almost fall off my chair. Smooth.

I managed to stand up and walk the few steps over to join Derek. He slung his arm over my shoulders.

"Okay, now what?" he asked Gary.

Gary stopped messing with his camera and looked up. "Um, I don't know," he said. "Do something that, like, works for your characters. You know—something that will look cool in a picture."

Derek looked sort of uncertain. "Okay," he said. "I guess we could, like, pretend we're dancing together or something. What do you think, Maggie?"

"I . . . uh . . . whu . . . ," I said with my usual eloquence. Why, oh why, did my vocal chords stop working whenever I was within six feet of Derek? Let alone less than six inches, as I was now. Why couldn't I seem to summon up any of the confidence and expressiveness I felt onstage?

I decided my only hope was to try to channel that by pretending I was in rehearsals. I needed to turn into Sally. Sally would know what to do.

I closed my eyes, reaching for the character. It wasn't easy. The sounds of clinking dishes and muffled salsa music rang out from the kitchen, and somewhere to our left some guys were talking loudly about a baseball game or something. That made it kind of hard to imagine myself at the Kit Kat Klub.

"Um, can you open your eyes, Maggie?" Gary called. "It'll look better in the picture."

My eyes flew open. I found both Gary and Derek staring at me. Shooting a glance at Calla for help, I saw her eating the rest of my grapes and gazing at me with concern.

"Hey, I have an idea," she called out. "Maybe you could pretend to dance like Derek said, and he could dip Maggie so she's sort of looking back upside down into the camera."

Thanks, Calla. That was all I needed in my current state—gymnastics.

Gary looked excited by the suggestion. "Ooh, that sounds really cool!" he exclaimed. "Do that, you guys!"

Derek shrugged. "Okay, let's give it a go," he said agreeably. Glancing at me, he smiled. "You trust me not to drop you on your head, right?"

A cheerleader would have giggled cutely. Calla would have retorted with some snappy comeback. But me? I just stared at him like a bunny caught in the headlights.

"Um," I said after a few seconds. "Okay. I mean, yes. I t-trust you."

Derek chuckled. "You don't sound too sure," he joked. Then, without waiting for an answer, he sort of grabbed me in his arms.

How many times had I dreamed about this moment? Too many to count, and in too many ways to remember. Somehow, though, none of them had involved a nerdy freshman with a camera or the lingering smell of mac and cheese.

Still, I felt my heart beating faster. His arms felt just as strong and sure as I'd always imagined. His aftershave mingled with the faint scent of the apple he'd just eaten. The feel of him was so overwhelming that I guess

I got a little confused. For that moment, I became Fabulous Maggie from my daydreams. I did what she would do, which turned out to be wrapping both my arms around him and snuggling up against his strong, broad chest.

"Um, Maggie?" Gary called out, shattering the momentary spell. "Let him dip you, okay? He won't drop you."

I felt the blood rush to my face as I came back to reality. What was I *doing*? I didn't particularly care what Gary thought, but what about Derek? Here he was just trying to pose for a picture and I was practically mauling him!

Loosening my grip, I tried to jump back. But Derek was still holding onto me, so I just ended up kind of bouncing back against his arms and stepping on his foot.

"Ow!" he yelped. Then he laughed. "Okay, hang on. Let's get organized here . . ."

Somehow, we positioned ourselves and got the photo. At least I'm pretty sure we did. I spent the whole time praying that he really would drop me on my head while I was upside down. Maybe that would knock some sense into me.

"Argh!" I cried as my voice cracked—again—on the high note near the end of the show's title song. "I just can't hit that one!"

"You can do it. You just need to let go and trust yourself to hit it." Nico tapped out the note on the music-room piano. "Try it again."

I sighed. It was Saturday afternoon, and we'd already been at it for more than an hour and a half. I wasn't sure how Nico had procured the keys to the music suite, or permission to be there on weekends. But I wasn't going to ask. "Don't you have somewhere to be? Band practice or work or something?" I asked him, remembering him mentioning something about that at the beginning of our session.

"Are you trying to get rid of me?"

"No!" I blurted out before noticing his sly little half smile and realizing he was joking. I blew out a sigh. "Um, sorry. Guess I'm just a little tense."

"It's okay." He stood up from the piano bench and stretched. He was wearing a slightly ratty old Ramones T-shirt, and as he stretched it rode up, revealing a slice of his lanky torso. He had pretty nice abs for such a skinny guy. I looked away quickly, feeling weird about noticing something like that.

"So what am I supposed to do if I can't hit that note?" I asked.

He finished stretching and blinked at me. "You can hit it," he said. "Your range is better than you think."

"Maybe." I chewed on my lower lip, feeling all my worries about the show welling up inside me. "But anyway, hitting one note is the least of my problems. Ms. Dana said we're going to start choreographing our dances soon. After that, it's only a matter of time before she'll expect me to sing and dance at the same time. What then? I still can't sing with my eyes open."

"Oh, is that why you've been looking so freaked out for the past couple of days?" Nico took a step toward me. "Okay, then let's deal with that."

Before I could wonder when he'd decided I was freaked out, he was standing right in front of me, holding out his hand. "Um, what are you doing?" I asked.

"You're worried about singing and dancing at the same time, right?" he replied. "Then come on, let's try it. Let's dance."

I blinked, not quite understanding for a second. Then he held out his other hand too, and I got it. He wanted us to dance together. Gulp. Dancing, abs, his noticing how I was feeling—what was going on here, anyway? Once again, I thought back to Calla's theory that Nico might be interested in more than a student-teacher relationship.

"Come on, don't leave me hanging, dude," he joked.

I smiled and relaxed. Okay, all my anxiety about Derek was clearly making me paranoid. Nico wasn't making a pass at me. He was just trying to help, as usual. I had to trust him. He'd been right about everything I needed to do so far.

"Okay, let's dance," I agreed, taking one of his hands in my own. His palm felt cool and smooth.

He wrapped his other arm around my waist. Then he hummed out a note. "Let's try doing 'Don't Tell Mama,'" he said. "I'll sing the Kit Kat Girls' part."

I closed my eyes, allowing him to lead. We twirled around the room in a crazy sort of combination waltz and tango. I sang the beginning of the song on my own. The first time he picked up the Girls' part in a shrill but pitch-perfect falsetto, I burst out laughing and opened my eyes. He started laughing too—so hard that his eyes squinted almost shut and his cheek twitched. I hadn't ever seen him laugh out loud like that. Usually he was more of a sardonic smirk kind of guy. He looked so different and so funny, it made me laugh even harder, and when I tried to control myself, I just ended up snorting like a rhinoceros. That made *him* laugh harder, and we just stood there clinging to each other for a while until we recovered.

"Um, okay," I gasped out at last. "Do you think maybe you could, like, sing the part an octave lower or something? The falsetto is, um, a little distracting." I stifled another giggle as I remembered it.

"Whatever you say," he replied with a grin. "Let's take it from the 'sweet patater' line, okay?"

Someday, when I'm a famous actress, an interviewer will probably ask me to describe the most embarrassing moment of my acting career. And now I know exactly what moment I'll think of first. Thanks, Ms. Dana.

It all started at our first dance rehearsal. We'd been rehearsing everything else for more than a week at that point, and it had been going fairly well. The blocking was pretty much set, we were all getting comfortable with our lines and characters, and even the singing was going okay so far.

Since we had rehearsals almost every day after school, most of my lessons with Nico had moved to lunchtime, study halls, and weekends. I even met him once or twice at the Thornton Diner, the popular local hangout where he had a part-time job. The Dumpster out back gave an interesting echo effect to our sessions, though the smell of day-old tuna salad and rotting vegetables didn't add much.

But no matter where we worked, I was making progress. Sure, I still couldn't sing with my eyes open for more than a few notes. But Nico said I was sounding better all the time. And since we hadn't started dance rehearsals yet, I was able to get away with just standing there onstage and singing my songs with my eyes closed.

Basically, aside from the occasional wacky improv exercise (Perform a rap song in character! Switch roles when I call out "swap!" Pretend to be a tree, a fish, a bowl of oatmeal!), it was pretty smooth sailing. For the first time, I was starting to truly believe

I just might survive this experience.

And then there was Derek. We were really starting to click, though only during rehearsals—whenever I encountered him off-stage, I still turned into Mushmouth Maggie, Mistress of Mumbles. But I was trying not to worry about that, because whenever we rehearsed our scenes together onstage, it was an entirely different story. It wasn't quite *Romeo and Juliet*, but it was close.

But back to that first dance rehearsal. I should probably start by pointing out that it was a total surprise to all of us. It turned out that Nico had a dentist appointment or something, so Ms. Dana had decided that instead of a regular rehearsal we might as well start learning choreography that day instead of the next as scheduled.

"Oh, great. I'm not exactly dressed for dancing practice," I muttered to Calla, smoothing out the short, flouncy skirt I was wearing. I'd chosen my outfit carefully that morning, thinking about another afternoon of acting opposite Derek.

Calla shrugged sympathetically. "It's okay," she said. "I'm not exactly *built* for dancing practice."

I knew she was just kidding around, trying to make me feel better. Other than a bit of waltzing and swaying with Herr Schultz, Fraulein Schneider didn't have to do any real dancing in the show.

"We're going to start with the most challenging dance first," Ms. Dana announced cheerfully. "Now, how many of you have seen the movie version of *Cabaret*?"

Most of the assembled cast raised their hands. Ms. Dana nodded, seeming pleased.

"Good. Then I'm sure you'll remember the song called 'Mein Herr' where the performers dance using chairs as props. Now, that particular song didn't even appear in the original stage show back in the sixties— it was written for the film. But the number was such a success that it was added to most later stage revivals of the show, and that's why we're doing it here."

I gulped. I did remember the number in question. Even before I'd had any idea I would be playing Sally, I'd commented to Calla and Duane that the chair dance looked impressively tricky.

"So are *we* going to dance with chairs too?" called out Lizzy Paolini, who was one of the Kit Kat Girls.

"Yes indeed. And I've had some expert

help in choreographing our version. Come on out here, Molly!" Ms. Dana turned and waved toward the back of the auditorium. I looked and saw Molly Kim, an energetic senior who was captain of the cheerleading squad and also cocaptain of the competitive dance team.

"Hi, guys," she cried out in her loud, high-pitched cheerleader voice as she bounded down the aisle toward the stage. "Come on. Everyone who's in this scene get up there so we can get started. This is going to be a blast! I didn't have time to try out for the musical myself, but at least this way I get to be in it in spirit!"

She let out a little whoop and did a graceful jump and kick thing. I guessed it was supposed to be some kind of cheer. I wouldn't know. Whenever I attended Thornton football games, I didn't spend much time watching the cheerleaders. I always kept my gaze trained firmly where it belonged—on Derek.

"Bring out the chairs, guys!" Ms. Dana yelled. Right on cue, several members of the stage crew appeared carrying wooden straight-back chairs.

Molly jumped onstage, where she immediately grabbed a chair and started ordering us around, showing us the moves while Ms. Dana picked out the melody of the song on the piano. Whenever we didn't move quite fast enough for her taste, Molly ran over and positioned our arms and legs and heads wherever they were supposed to be, grinning maniacally the whole time. She was kind of intimidating. No, scratch that—she was terrifying!

Like I said, I'm not a bad dancer. I'd taken some classes in my time, done my share of Dance Dance Revolution in Calla's living room, and busted plenty of moves at school dances (mostly trying to attract Derek's attention, not that it ever worked). But this dance was something else. Basically, I was supposed to sing most of the song while perching in various weird and awkward poses atop one of those wooden chairs. By the time we'd been practicing for twenty minutes, I was out of breath and my thighs were screaming for mercy.

"Hang on," I gasped as I jumped up on the chair, standing on the seat with one foot while propping the other on the back, doing my best not to flash the audience at the same time by holding down the edges of my skirt. "Am I doing this right?"

Molly turned away from helping Jenna Paolini balance on her side across the seat of her chair and shot me a critical glance. "Almost," she barked out. "Lean forward more. More!"

"Um, are you sure?" I tried to do as she said, but hesitated as I felt the chair wobble alarmingly beneath me. "It's kind of precarious . . ."

"It's supposed to look precarious," Molly retorted. "That's what makes it interesting."

I heard a ripple of laughter from the audience. Ms. Dana had said that anyone who didn't have a dancing part could leave early, but most people had stayed behind to watch. Among them was—gulp—Derek.

Trying not to wonder if he could see up my skirt, I focused on Molly. "Um, okay," I said. "I guess . . ."

"Try singing the song while you do it, Maggie," Ms. Dana suggested from her seat in the front row. "Doing something familiar and comfortable like that may help take your mind off the new stuff."

Yeah, right. If only she knew . . .

But what could I do? If I didn't take her advice, she'd probably force me to do some exercise to put me in touch with my inner chair dancer. So I stood there, legs trembling, and sang one of the verses of the song. Well, *tried* to sing it, anyway. The first note came out sounding horrible. Automatically, my eyes snapped shut. Whew! That was better. My voice stabilized immediately. I imagined Nico saying "Pitch. Pitch. Good!" as I found the melody.

And what do you know, Ms. Dana was right. Focusing on my singing made me forget all about what I was doing.

Unfortunately, what I was doing was balancing precariously on a wobbly old chair. As I leaned forward, stretching for one of the notes, I suddenly felt the world tip sideways.

"Oh!" I exclaimed, my eyes flying open.

But it was too late. I'd leaned forward a bit too far, and my chair was tumbling over backward. I scrambled, trying to jump free, but my foot skidded on the smooth, worn wooden surface of the seat and slipped through the slats of the chair back. I was stuck!

"Aaaaah!" I cried as the back of the chair

hit the floor with a loud crash. A second later my body landed with an even louder thud. That was going to leave a bruise.

But that was the least of my worries. My foot was still stuck, which meant I couldn't stand up or even move very much, at least not without gnawing off my own foot. And that actually seemed like kind of a tempting option, given that my skirt was somewhere up over my waist and I was flashing the entire auditorium with my pink lace-trimmed panties.

Twelve

That proved it once and for all. It really *wasn't* possible to die of embarrassment. Because if it were, that moment would have been fatal for sure.

"Are you okay?" someone yelled.

"Maggie! What happened?" Molly exclaimed loudly.

Other people were calling out as well. But all I could hear through the din was one voice: "Hold still, Maggie. I've got you."

It was Derek. I frantically shoved my skirt more or less back into place, then just lay there, wishing that spontaneous human combustion was for real so I could give it a try. At least that might be surprising enough to make everyone forget what had just happened. Otherwise my gravestone would surely read:

MAGGIE TANNERY, CLUMSY ACTRESS

HER PANTIES WERE HER TRAGIC DOWNFALL

Seconds later Derek's gorgeous face was hovering above me, looking concerned. "Can you move your toes? Do you think you broke anything?"

"Uh, yeah. I mean, no. I mean, I'm fine." I sent an urgent mental message to Calla, begging her to rush onstage and knock Derek out with one of the chairs. Once he was unconscious, I figured we could decide which memory-erasing drug to use to ensure he'd never remember this humiliating moment.

Oh, but wait. This was real life, not one of my fantasies. So that probably wasn't going to work. I struggled helplessly against the stupid chair.

"Wait, hold still a sec." I felt Derek's strong hands on my ankle. I was so distracted by trying to remember when I'd last shaved my legs that I was hardly aware of what he was doing. Before I knew it, my leg was free.

"Th-thanks," I stammered, sitting up and glancing down to make sure everything was covered that should be.

"No problem." He smiled at me and held out a hand to help me up. "And, hey, you were looking pretty good up there. You know—before, um . . ." He glanced at the fallen chair, shrugged, and grinned.

I did my best to paste on a good-natured grin in response. Guys like a girl with a sense of humor, right?

"Good!" Nico said, sounding satisfied. "That sounded much better. I think you've got it."

I opened my eyes and smiled at him. "Thanks."

It was Friday afternoon. Luckily, Nico and I had the same study hall schedule. There was a sophomore music-appreciation class in the main music room at the moment, so we were stuck with one of the practice rooms, which wasn't much bigger than a coat closet. With no piano, Nico had resorted to accompanying me on acoustic guitar. It was actually pretty cool. The smaller room and the different sound of the guitar gave a relaxed and cozy feel to our practice. I was even feeling comfortable enough to really go for the high note in the show's title song— and the last time through, I'd actually hit and held it.

Nico strummed out another chord. "Okay," he said, smiling back at me. "One more time from the top . . ."

A couple of days later, I was still brooding over the Great Chair-Falling Incident. For one thing, I'd made a vow never to wear a skirt again, at least not without Bermuda shorts underneath. As Calla, Duane, and I sat down at our usual table in the cafeteria, I spotted Derek across the room coming out of the lunch line with a group of his jock buddies. He wasn't looking at me, but I felt myself blush.

"I still can't believe it," I murmured. "Why did he have to stick around to witness my humiliation? He doesn't have to dance—he could've left."

"Snap out of it, babe." Calla jabbed a straw into her diet soda. "You're not the only one with problems."

Duane shot her a look. "Did you ask Glenn about rehearsing with you privately like I suggested?" he asked her.

"Yeah." Calla shrugged and took a sip of the soda. "He said he'd do it. But when I tried to pin down a time and place, he blew me off and said we'd have to figure it out."

I blinked, suddenly realizing that I had no idea what they were talking about, and that Calla sounded kind of dejected. In other words, very un-Calla-like.

"Wait, is something wrong?" I asked. "Are you having trouble with your part? I thought you were great up there yesterday."

That was true, mostly. I'd been pretty busy anytime I wasn't onstage feeling self-conscious and sneaking looks at Derek to see if he was looking at me funny after the previous day's disaster. But I certainly hadn't noticed anything off about Calla's acting when I had been paying attention.

"Well, of course I was." Calla patted her hair, which had recently gone black with purple streaks. But then her hand dropped to the table and she sighed. "It's just, well, you know Glenn—I suppose I shouldn't let it bother me when he—"

"Hi there!" a new voice interrupted.

My head shot up so fast I almost flipped over backward. It was Derek. He was grinning at us, holding a loaded lunch tray.

"Well hi, handsome." Calla's moment of vulnerability was gone, and once again she was her usual bold, brassy self. "Looking for some hot mamas to sit with? Because we have three of them right here." She smirked at Duane, who rolled his eyes.

"Thanks. Don't mind if I do." Derek set down his tray and folded his long legs under the table as he took a seat. "See, I'm a little confused by what Ms. Dana means when she tells me to relate to my songs."

"Oh, really?" Calla pursed her lips and arched her eyebrows. "A smart boy like you confused by something like that? Come on, you can be honest with us. If you're looking for an excuse to get closer to my fabulousness, just say so."

Derek laughed, and Duane snorted. "You're breaking my heart, baby," he joked with a mock sob. "How can you flirt with your new boyfriend right in front of me?"

"Dude, you don't have to worry. I'd never scam on another guy's girl." Derek shot Calla a playful grin and a wink. "No matter how tempting it might be."

Calla patted her hair. "That's all right, you two don't need to fight. There's plenty of me to go around."

"Cool." Derek's grin faded. "But listen, I'm serious here. You guys know this whole acting thing is new to me. I really don't want to mess it up. . . ."

You may have noticed that I hadn't said anything yet. There was a reason for that. As usual, I'd gone mute in Derek's presence. He turned to glance at me, probably expecting me to act like I did when we were onstage together. You know—normal.

Fat chance. I tried to cover up my consternation by grabbing my tuna salad sandwich and taking a big bite. That should buy me a few seconds . . .

At the same time, I took a few deep breaths to steady myself. Oops. Bad idea. A chunk of tuna got sucked in and went down my windpipe.

I hacked discreetly, trying to dislodge it. No dice. Feeling my air cut off, I grabbed my throat, suddenly too busy panicking about choking to death to worry about what Derek might think. It was good to know something could take my mind off that, I guess.

Calla was the first to notice my predicament. "Mags! Are you okay?"

Derek glanced over again. "Oh man, is she choking? Maggie! Are you choking?"

I tried to wave my hands airily in an "Oh no, I'll be okay" sort of way. But it probably came off more like a desperate clawing at my fading life force.

Derek leaped to his feet, probably perfectly prepared to perform the Heimlich maneuver on me. The thought was so alarming that I coughed one last time, forcing the piece of tuna to finally pop out.

"I'm okay," I gasped as my breath returned with a whoosh. "I'm fine."

Technically speaking, though, "fine" might have been an overstatement. Why did I still turn into a total spaz whenever Derek was looking? It was like one of those curses where someone has everything except the one thing she desires most. In other words, not fair. Not fair at all.

After the embarrassing lunch incident, I was starting to resign myself to the fact that the stage was the only place I'd ever be able to have the relationship I dreamed of with Derek. At least I had that, I told myself, vowing to make the most of it.

When I walked into rehearsal that Friday, Ms. Dana had a certain gleam in her eye, one we were all starting to recognize. That gleam was like a big, neon beacon flashing out: WARNING! WARNING! GOOFY IMPROV EXERCISE DEAD AHEAD! PROCEED AT OWN RISK!

Sure enough, we all soon found ourselves

pretending to be kernels of popcorn in a hot pan. We were supposed to crouch down and wait until we thought we were "done," and then jump up, clap our hands, and yell "Pop!" at the top of our lungs. I stayed down as long as I could, wondering if these exercises were actually designed to make me look as silly as possible in front of Derek. Not that I wasn't doing a bang-up job of that myself . . .

"Excellent! Excellent!" Ms. Dana cried after a few minutes of popcorning. "Terrific warm-up, people. I can see by your attitudes about that little game that you're ready for what we're going to do today."

Uh-oh. I didn't like the sound of that.

"It's time." She beamed at us, as proud as a mama bear over her cubs. "You guys know your songs. You're getting better at your dances. So let's put this show together and see what we've got!"

"You mean sing and dance at the same time?" Jenna sounded nervous—though not a tenth as nervous as I felt.

Ms. Dana trilled out a giddy little laugh. "That's how it's done!" She clapped her hands. "Places, everyone. Act one, scene one. Nico?"

Nico was seated at the piano in the orchestra pit. At her cue, he started playing the intro of the opening song, "Willkommen."

We all scrambled to our spots. I was only part of the chorus at the end of "Willkommen," with no real dancing, so that gave me time to consider my options. As I saw it, they were as follows:

1. Figure out how to sing with my eyes open.
2. Figure out how to dance with my eyes closed.
3. Contact a witch doctor about acquiring a new personality, stat.

None of those options seemed particularly promising. I shot a look at Nico, who was bent over the piano keys playing away. We'd been working on the eyes-open thing off and on in our lessons, but hadn't made much progress. He'd tried that look-into-my-eyes thing again, but this time I kept thinking back to the time we'd danced together and couldn't stop giggling long enough to get more than two notes out. We'd also tried having me open my eyes for only the last word of every line. That had sort of worked at first. But about four or five lines in, I'd started getting confused and forgetting exactly when my eyes were supposed to be open or shut. After that, we'd both sort of given up and just worked on my phrasing in the title song for a while.

So now here I was, feeling like I was getting ready to jump out of a plane without a parachute. Not that I would ever put it that way when Ms. Dana was within earshot. She'd probably think that was a great idea for a new acting exercise.

After the opening song, I stepped backstage with the others while Derek, Tommy, and the sophomore kid played out the train scene. There was no singing in that one except for a little bit from Duane at the end, so it went by quickly.

One more scene, and then it's all me, I thought as the scene shifted to the boardinghouse and Calla and Derek started trading lines. Would this be the moment the whole world realized I wasn't up to this role? I shot another, slightly desperate glance at Nico, but he was paging through his music and didn't notice.

Anyway, there wasn't much he could do at this point. I was on my own. I distracted myself from that scary thought by tuning in as Calla started to sing her first song, "So What?" She sounded great—full-throated and confident, as usual. Despite my anxiety, I found myself smiling as I watched her moving effortlessly around the stage, bringing Fraulein Schneider to life. Derek stood and watched, perfectly embodying likable Cliff.

As the song ended, Bethany entered, playing Fraulein Kost, a woman of ill repute who also lived in the boardinghouse. And a few lines after that, here came Glenn as Herr Schultz.

We made fun of Glenn a lot, but he was actually a decent actor. True, he definitely seemed to prefer the more heroic roles—it was pretty obvious that he considered himself the good-looking leading-man type. But he'd clearly been working on getting into his current part as a meek older man, and came onstage with a slightly stooped, shuffling gait and a cheerful smile with just a hint of uncertainty. I was impressed.

I glanced at Calla, looking forward to seeing the two of them play off each other. The blocking called for Fraulein Schneider to put a hand on Herr Schultz's arm as she introduced him to the others in the scene. To my surprise, Calla looked tentative, barely touching Glenn's sleeve before dropping her hand and backing away. She delivered her next couple of lines normally, but when she was supposed to speak to Herr Schultz again, she stared out at the auditorium without so much as glancing at Glenn.

"Look at him, Calla," Ms. Dana called. "You're supposed to be flirting. Show it, my daisy!"

"Okay." Calla cleared her throat and spoke the lines again. This time she sort of edged closer to Glenn and glanced at him out of the corner of her eye. It was weird. Flirting came as naturally to Calla as breathing. Why wasn't she calling on that right now? Was this some kind of weird character study or something?

I was still puzzling over that one when the piano started up again and one of the girls in the chorus started pretending to sing into a telephone. That chased everything else out of my mind, because it meant my first song was coming up in just a few seconds. Yikes. How was I going to pull this off? I thought back to that one moment where I'd actually managed to sing with my eyes open, that day with Nico. That had been a duet, but still . . . Glancing down at his head bent over the piano keys, I took a deep breath, trying to summon up some Sally Bowles–like confidence. If I'd done it once, I could do it again. Maybe this would be the moment when I finally proved that.

I strode out right on cue, remembering how Molly had taught me to "walk like I meant it." That part went okay. A couple of the guys watching from the audience even let out appreciative hoots and whistles, though Ms. Dana shushed them quickly. I just smiled, for that moment feeling very Sally-esque. Grabbing an imaginary microphone (the props crew was still working on getting us the stuff we needed), I opened my mouth to sing the opening line of the song.

And . . . nothing came out. I quickly closed my eyes. Whew! There it was. The song poured out of me, just as I'd sung it a dozen times before.

A couple of lines in, Ms. Dana called for a cut. "Don't just stand there, Maggie!" she said. "We're putting it together with the dance, remember?"

Oh, I remembered all right. I moistened

my lips as Nico started the intro chords again, forcing myself not to look around and see if Derek was watching me. This was it. Trial by fire.

Once again, as soon as I tried to sing with my eyes open, my throat closed up, refusing to let a single note escape. I covered it up by coughing and then immediately closing my eyes and singing. I shuffled around a bit, doing some lame little version of the dance steps. But I knew I couldn't get away with that for long—Ms. Dana might be weird, but as far as I knew, her eyesight was perfectly normal. It was only a matter of time before she noticed that the reason I was dancing like a doofus was that my eyes were shut tight.

Figuring I might have better luck now that I was actually rolling, I carefully opened one eye. For a second I thought it was going to work—the words and notes kept coming, probably due to sheer momentum. However, within half a line they started fading out, going all squeaky and off-key. Yikes!

"Cut!" I called out, the other eye popping open. I'd just had an idea. It wouldn't solve my problem in the long term, but at least it might get me through this rehearsal.

After that I would have to put my head together with Nico and figure something out. "Um, Ms. Dana, I was, um, thinking about, you know, my character? And I was wondering, um, that is, I had an idea for . . . for an acting exercise to help me get, you know, more in touch with her?"

"Yes?" Ms. Dana perked up immediately at her favorite words, "acting exercise." "What is it, Maggie?"

"I was wondering if I could wear sunglasses during today's rehearsal," I said, ignoring the murmurs and strange looks from my fellow actors, who probably thought I'd suddenly lost my mind and joined Ms. Dana's Kult of Krazee Acting Krap. "Um, to show that Sally, uh, sees the disturbing events happening all around her in prewar Berlin through a haze of denial within her own mind."

The murmurs from behind me were getting louder. But Ms. Dana looked ecstatic. "I think that's an excellent idea, Maggie!" she exclaimed. "I appreciate your initiative and your questing spirit. Let's give it a try."

Soon I was back onstage with my darkest shades hiding my eyes from the outside world. Now Ms. Dana would have no idea my eyes were still closed while I sang. The only thing I had to figure out was how to do just enough dancing to keep her happy without killing myself.

Oh, well, it wasn't as if we were Broadway pros. If I just kept shuffling around, I figured she'd cut me some slack since this was our first time.

We took it again from the top. The first part went pretty smoothly. I stubbed my toe against the boards once and almost tripped, but caught myself.

Then the Kit Kat Girls came in on their part. It was kind of unnerving hearing them singing behind me and knowing that they were moving around back there. I opened my eyes to peek a few times during pauses in my part, not wanting to get too close. Yikes! Just in time. I dodged as Lizzy flung her arm out, almost decapitating me.

Darting to a safer distance, I closed my eyes again as my next part came up. At this point in the song I was supposed to start dancing my way over toward Cliff, who was sitting at the far end of the stage at one of the little round tables in the Kit Kat Klub. We didn't have actual tables yet, so we were making do with overturned buckets, stacks of books, and large cardboard boxes.

I sneaked a peek during a breath and saw Derek sitting there watching me. How could a six-foot guy perched on a bucket look so crazy hot? It distracted me so much that I came in late on my next line, forgot to close my eyes for a second, and hit a note that sounded as if it came from another dimension. Snapping my eyes shut, I fished for the right note—and found it. Whew! I could almost hear Nico in my head saying, "Nice save!"

"Dance over to Cliff's table, Maggie!" Ms. Dana called. "You're supposed to be singing directly to him now."

I obeyed, scooting in the direction of where Derek was sitting. At least I thought it was the direction of where Derek was sitting. I started to wonder when my knee banged into something that felt suspiciously like the suitcase prop that was supposed to be backstage at this point. "Don't Tell Mama" was a fast-paced song, and the beat was driving me along, making it hard to stop and think. I jumped aside as I sang and (sort of) danced, trying to gauge which way I should go. Shouldn't I have had some kind of radar by now, some sixth sense that told me exactly where Derek was at all times?

If I did, it must have been low on batteries or something. Because the next thing I knew, my foot hit something hard that almost immediately gave way.

"Ow!" I blurted out, dropping the song in the middle of a line as my eyes flew open. I'd staggered right into one of the stacks of books that was serving as a chair, though luckily nobody was sitting on it at the time. Trying to catch myself to keep from tripping, I stepped right onto one of the books. It skidded out from under my foot and I started to do an involuntary split. That only increased my panic. Given my luck lately, it took only a fraction of a second to fully envision my pants splitting and my underwear once again on full display. With a great effort of will, I heaved myself back to my feet—just in time to wobble and fall over right onto the cardboard-box table in front of Derek.

I lay there, stunned, staring up into his surprised face. Nico had stopped playing, and the Kit Kat Girls were silent as well.

"Well," Ms. Dana spoke up after what

seemed like an endless gulf of time but was probably only a second or two. "That was very, er, dramatic, Maggie. But maybe next time through you should stick to the choreography we practiced, all right?"

Thirteen

A week later, I was still clamming up and going all weird every time I saw Derek outside of rehearsals. However, onstage was another matter. After I'd demolished the Kit Kat Klub, Ms. Dana had decided we needed a few more dance-only practices before putting everything together. Once I could go back to singing with my eyes closed without endangering myself or others, everything was fine.

Actually, more than fine. Much more. The way Derek looked at me during our scenes together, the way he touched me—it was as if it wasn't carefully blocked out and stage-directed at all, but just two people falling in love despite the chaos and uncertainty of the world around them. I'd never felt anything like it. It took my breath away. Again, I'd always thought that was just an expression. But the first time we practiced our kissing scenes, I found out just how true it was.

See, Sally Bowles is the type of person who doesn't hesitate to kiss someone. Throughout the play she kisses people hello, and kisses Cliff numerous times—including the first time they meet. Up until that point, we'd been handling all the kisses as pecks on the cheek. That had been mind-blowing enough. The first time I'd been ordered to plant a smackerooni on Derek's perfectly chiseled cheekbone, I'd almost passed out. And the first time he'd bent down to kiss me on the forehead in that New Year's Eve scene, it had been a real struggle to remember my next line and stay in character. Still, it helped somehow that everyone sort of giggled every time, like overgrown second graders on the playground, including me and Derek. It made it seem less real somehow. Less important.

But now Ms. Dana wanted us to take it to the next level. "Okay, let's stop being goofy about this," she told Derek after one such cheek kiss. "Your audience wants to believe with you. That means you must give them something believable. In this scene, Cliff is showing that meeting Sally is already inspiring him to become more impulsive than his nature. He should give her a real kiss." She fluttered both hands in the air. "So show me something real, you two. I know you can do it! You have the rest of the emotion down pat. So let us see that reflected in your kiss!"

"Okay." Derek glanced at me and winked. "You okay with this?"

I couldn't speak. So I just nodded. What else was I going to do? Even if my voice was working properly, it wouldn't sound too good to admit that I was afraid I might faint the moment his lips touched mine, like some kind of psychotic opposite-world version of *Sleeping Beauty*. I also wasn't about to explain that this wouldn't *really* be our first real kiss, since we'd sucked face like crazy at least a million times in my fantasies.

So I just gave my line and then waited. Derek gave his lines, then interrupted himself with a smile. "Happy New Year," he said, leaning over and tilting his head. A second later I felt his lips press against mine. They felt surprisingly soft and smooth.

My eyes fluttered shut, and I melted into the kiss. For those few, fleeting seconds I wasn't myself, I wasn't Sally, I was just a part of that magical moment with him. Then he pulled away, and my eyes opened again automatically.

"I'm Sally Bowles," I began, chattering on as scripted, as if I hadn't just shared a timeless moment with the man of my dreams. And when I was supposed to kiss him a little later in the scene, it didn't take any prompting from Ms. Dana for me to plant one on him. This scene was Sally trying playfully to shock Cliff, while at the same time showing that she liked him. So we lingered a bit longer over the kiss, and I allowed my hands to wander over his neck and shoulders in a very Sally-like (and un-Maggie-like) way.

"Excellent!" Ms. Dana exclaimed when I finally pulled away and delivered my next line, only a little breathless. "That was superb, you two. I really believed in your emotional connection! Let's try it again. This time, Maggie, I want you to touch his face as you pull away, and let your hand linger . . ."

We ended up practicing that kiss about three more times. I certainly wasn't complaining, and Derek didn't seem to mind, either. *Romeo and Juliet?* We didn't need no stinkin' *Romeo and Juliet*. . . .

I was still floating on air as I hurried down the stage steps to the auditorium floor a few minutes later. Duane and a couple of the Kit Kat Girls had just started their next song, but I hardly heard them. Flopping into the seat beside Calla, I let out a blissful sigh.

"Did you get a load of that?" I whispered to her.

"Uh-huh." Calla was examining her bright pink fingernails.

I shot her a look. She sounded kind of down. In other words, very un-Calla-like.

"Are you okay?" I asked.

"I don't know." She grimaced. "Why don't you ask Glenn?"

"Huh?"

At first I was confused. Then I belatedly remembered that weird little half conversation between her and Duane at lunch a while back, and also the way she'd sort of dropped out of character during the scene with Glenn the previous week.

"Hang on," I said. "Calla, what's going

on? Are you having trouble with Glenn or something?"

"Who, me?" She shrugged and wriggled her shoulders expressively. "Since when do I have a problem with a man?"

It was a typical Calla response. Still, I frowned, not quite liking the lingering un-Calla-like look in her eyes. Before I could press her, Ms. Dana called my name.

"Back onstage, please," the director said. "I'd like to go back and run scene four again. There are a few things I'd like to try before we quit for today."

My heart jumped. Running the scene again meant more kissing with Derek. And that was something I didn't mind repeating, even if it meant running past quitting time. In fact, I'd be perfectly happy if the entire show consisted of the two of us just standing there making out for a couple of hours. With musical accompaniment, of course.

"We'll talk about this later," I told Calla distractedly, already heading back toward the stage.

"Come on." Nico sounded kind of frustrated. "It's just the two of us. Open your stupid eyes and sing already."

"I can't help it." I frowned at him. "This isn't easy for me, you know. It's not like I'm doing it on purpose to annoy you."

He shook his head and snorted. It was clear he was losing patience with me. We'd been working again on trying to get me to sing with my eyes open, but as usual it wasn't going too well.

"Look, we've got to figure out how to break you out of this," he said. "Ms. Dana said we're going to try a full run-through of the first act tomorrow. That means you're going to have to sing and dance without spazzing out and destroying the scenery."

"Gee, way to be supportive."

He scowled. "You don't need support right now. What you need is to just do this. And we don't have much time—I'm supposed to be at the diner for my shift in, like, half an hour." He raked his hands through his hair, making the spikes spikier than ever. "Look, the staring thing worked that one time before, and the dancing thing sort of almost worked. Let's try combining them. After all, if you can't move and sing with your eyes open, you'll never get through this show."

"Fine, okay. You know best, right?" It

came out a little more sarcastic than I'd intended.

He stepped over and punched a button on his iPod, which was hooked up to some tiny but high-tech-looking speakers. The opening notes of "Perfectly Marvelous" poured out, sounding surprisingly rich and full.

"What, you don't want to channel the Kit Kat Girls today by doing 'Don't Tell Mama'?" I joked weakly, trying to lighten the mood.

"Don't talk. Don't laugh." He grabbed me around the waist and swung me toward him, gripping my hand in his. "Just dance— and sing. Eyes on me."

He sort of glowered down at me. I stared back at him, trying to muster up some of Sally's bravado. I was starting to wonder if Nico was the type of guy who enjoyed banging his head against the wall. Because just about anyone else would have given up on me by now. Even Calla and Duane were starting to sound a little insincere when they assured me I'd pull it together before opening night.

My cue came up, and I started to sing. The first note was pretty pathetic, but Nico hummed loudly, pulling me back on key.

Once I got there, he dropped out and just listened, dancing and looking at me.

And I mean really *looking* at me. It was unnerving. But his X-ray eyes seemed to do the trick, distracting me just enough that I forgot I couldn't sing with my eyes open and just did it.

Then it was time for Cliff's part of the song. Nico came in right on cue, his voice very different than Derek's, but still as smooth as butter. He sang the lines as if he truly meant them. I was so surprised by how effortlessly he captured the part of a lovelorn fellow acting against his better instincts that I almost missed my own next line.

I picked it up a word or two late. But that didn't matter. The notes were there, pure and strong. We finished up, singing the final line together. As the music ended, Nico laughed out loud.

"You did it!" There was no hint of the world-weary punk now; he sounded as delighted as a little boy. "Way to go, Maggie—you totally killed it! See? I knew you could do it!"

He grabbed me and hugged me. I laughed breathlessly and hugged him back. He was right. I'd done it!

Then both of us suddenly seemed to realize what we were doing. We pulled apart and stared at each other sort of sheepishly. There was a moment of awkward silence.

Then I brushed a lock of hair out of my face, wanting to smooth this over before he got all weird and angry again. "Um, but how do I transfer it over to the stage tomorrow?" I asked tentatively. "Do you really think I can do it?"

"Let's test it. Sing it again—this time on your own." He stepped back and hit the start button again on his iPod.

Taking a deep breath, I waited for my cue. It was a little harder picking up the first line without Nico's help, and it came out a little wobbly. But I bore down and kept trying, eyes wide open. After all, I'd done it before. The only thing stopping me from a repeat performance was myself. And I wasn't going to let myself stop me. Not this time.

By midway through the second verse, I was grinning like a fool. I was doing it. *I was doing it!*

Nico looked equally thrilled. As Cliff's part came in he started singing it again. And somehow, before I knew it, we were back to dancing together. This time he didn't bother to take my hand. He just wrapped both arms around my waist, and I lifted my own arms to his shoulders and sang up to him with a smile.

He gazed down at me with an expression of sheer adoration, and my heart started beating a little faster. I reminded myself that he was just acting, pretending to be Cliff, probably to test me to make sure I wouldn't get distracted once I was acting and singing and dancing all at the same time. So I did my best to throw myself into Sally as wholeheartedly as I did onstage with Derek. I sang to Cliff, putting all of Sally's hope and attraction and optimism into my voice. Cliff responded in kind, singing earnestly back to me while pulling me closer until our bodies were touching. I could feel his heart beating against my chest, and I rested my head against his shoulder. . . .

Suddenly I sort of popped back out of character, like one of those popcorn kernels in Ms. Dana's crazy exercise. What was going on here? My vocals chords stuttered to a halt midnote. I was feeling too confused to even try picking it up again. Why was I suddenly having these . . . these . . . these Derek-like feelings for Nico? Why did I have the urge to play out the rest of the scene, including the kiss at the end of it?

"What's wrong? Lose your place?" Nico murmured, still swaying to the music. He pulled me even closer, wrapping both arms around me and softly singing my part.

That was too much for me. I stopped dancing and yanked myself loose of his grip. "There," I said a little too loudly, taking several big steps backward until he was once again at a safe distance. "I did it. Now all I have to do is repeat it tomorrow for real. You know—with Derek." Derek's name came out even louder than the rest of it, and I tried to cover up my consternation with a nervous laugh. "You know, you're a better actor than I thought. Thanks for helping out."

He stood there staring at me for a moment, his hands crammed in the pockets of his jeans and his dark eyes unreadable. "Right. I'm quite an actor." Turning away, he started gathering up his iPod and other things. "Guess we're done here. See you tomorrow."

Fourteen

At first I thought that weird little scene with Nico had been all for nothing. The next day, as threatened, Ms. Dana announced that we would be running the first act start to finish, complete with dancing. Nico was late because of having to make up a quiz, so she had us sing our songs a cappella until he arrived, with only a plunked-out opening note or two to keep us on key. Duane and the Kit Kat Girls did fine with that, as did Calla. But when it was time for me to stride onstage and belt out "Don't Tell Mama," it was the same as it ever was—I squeaked out a couple of horrible off-key notes and was ready to run away and never come back. Or at least close my eyes and take my risks with the laws of physics.

Just then I heard the squeak of the auditorium's sticky side door opening. Glancing over, desperate for anything to take my mind off my own humiliation, I saw Nico hurrying in.

And just like that, my voice was back. I started over, this time nailing the opening line of the song. And what do you know— with my eyes open, I was able to nail the dance steps too, and even avoid falling off the stage at the same time. Funny how that works! Glancing down at Nico again after the first verse, I saw that he was smiling. When I caught his eye, he shot me a thumbs-up. Then he hurried over to the piano. Ms. Dana slid aside to let him take her place on the bench, and Nico's slim fingers flew over the keys, effortlessly picking up the accompaniment and playing along with me.

It wasn't until the scene was over and I was backstage waiting for my next cue that I realized what had happened out there. It was Nico. I hadn't been able to sing, and then he'd come in, and my voice had returned just like that. He was my magic talisman, my Dumbo's feather, my key to musical success.

Weird. I mean, yeah, Nico was the one who'd taught me to sing in the first place. But it wasn't as if I needed all my original teachers around to accomplish anything. Mr. Fayne was the one who'd taught me to act, and as much as I still missed him every day, I was doing okay without him. My parents had taught me to speak and dress myself, and I was able to carry on a coherent discussion or tie my shoes even when they were nowhere in sight.

So what was so different about this? I didn't know, and at the moment, I didn't really care that much. The bottom line was, I needed Nico: laser-beam eyes, weird moments, Ramones T-shirts, and all. As long as he was around—and luckily, he was, most of the time—I would be able to perform and avoid embarrassing myself in front of the world, especially my favorite new kissing partner, Derek.

And wasn't that all that really mattered?

A week later, it was still working. I hardly ever got anxious about my songs anymore. As long as I could catch a glimpse of Nico at the piano before I started, I was able to sing and dance with confidence—and wide-open eyes.

Better yet, that newfound confidence was allowing me to click even more with Derek. The two of us were becoming closer and more in synch than ever, though naturally it was still mostly confined to the stage. Even in the scenes where Cliff and Sally argued, we always seemed to end up smiling at each other.

"No!" Ms. Dana cried as we finished a scene near the end of the first act. "I realize you two just got engaged. But it is not a happy moment. Neither of you is sure you are doing the right thing. Cliff, you especially are very anxious—you are being forced to smuggle for the Nazis, after all! Think how that would feel. Now try it again!"

"Fine." Derek winked at me, then blinked and took on a serious expression. "This time through I'll try to focus on the Nazis rather than the pretty girl."

I giggled and blushed and dropped a playful little curtsy. Yeah, that was Sally reacting, obviously. If I'd been Maggie at the moment, I probably would have tripped and fallen on him or something.

Then both Sally and Maggie noticed Ms. Dana's expression. I quickly gulped back another giggle, not wanting her pulling out her Big Book of Acting Exercises again. We ran the end of the scene once more, and this time she seemed more or less satisfied.

"Nice," Derek murmured as we wandered backstage. Duane rushed past us, taking the stage to perform his next song. But I hardly noticed. I was focused on Derek. He walked back to a private spot behind some cables and stuff, then turned to face me and said it again. "That was really nice."

"Yeah," I said. "It was." I wasn't even sure what we were talking about. Nevertheless, I couldn't help agreeing with him.

He reached out and gave my upper arm a soft squeeze. "You know, I'm really glad you're playing Sally," he said. "It's been great acting with you, Maggie—and getting to know you. You're the perfect girl to introduce me to this whole crazy acting gig, and I can't imagine doing this show without you."

"Yeah," I stammered. "Um, I mean, me too. I mean, you're perfect. Uh, I mean, great. Too. Uh . . ."

As usual, Sally had fled as soon as we left center stage, leaving behind only tongue-tied Maggie. Derek was still gazing at me, seeming not to notice that I wasn't making much sense.

"What are you doing back here?" Glenn hissed at me as he hurried past. "Pay attention. You need to come on right after our song."

I blinked, snapping out of it. Glancing out toward the stage, I saw that Duane was just finishing his number.

"Oops, he's right," I said, a bit relieved by the interruption. On the one hand, having Derek say sweet things to me was, well, pretty much my dream come true with a cherry on top. On the other hand, once again it seemed to have taken me by surprise. I didn't want to blow it by acting like a moron. "Um, I need to go watch so I'll be ready for my cue."

Hurrying to the edge of the stage, I saw that Duane had just exited on the other side. Calla and Bethany were playing out the beginning of the next scene, in which Fraulein Kost catches Fraulein Schneider letting Herr Schultz out of her bedroom.

I smiled as I watched Calla act her part with gusto, remembering belatedly—and with a touch of guilt—that I'd never followed up on her weird mood a while back. *Oh well*, I thought. *Whatever it was, I guess she got over it.*

Then Glenn stepped forward as Herr Schultz to defend her honor. Facing down the smug Fraulein Kost, he reached out and put an arm around Calla's waist. And as soon as he touched her, it was as if Calla sort of . . . *wilted* right before my eyes, becoming smaller and paler and quieter, like a deflated balloon. The rest of her lines were delivered in close to a monotone and without any of her usual verve or volume.

"Release, Calla!" Ms. Dana called. That seemed to be her word for the week. She'd said it to me several times already that afternoon, along with a bunch of other theater-major mumbo jumbo, like "let your inner Sally Bowles take over" and "find the passion in the part." Now she continued, "You're supposed to be embarrassed, yes, but also happy. Herr Schultz has just proposed!"

"Sorry," Calla said dully. She tried again, but her lines fell just as flat.

"Never mind." Ms. Dana stood up and clapped her hands. "I think we've been rehearsing too hard, perhaps getting a bit stale. Let's try something to shake us up a bit . . ."

There were a few groans from around the auditorium. We all knew what that meant.

Sure enough, within moments we were all flapping our "wings" and running around the stage squawking while Ms. Dana kept shouting "Release!" at us. I sneaked several glances at Derek as I flapped around, my face going pink every time he caught my eye. And only partly from remembering that moment between us backstage. It was mostly because none of my fantasies about getting to know him better had involved playing crazy birdie games, or pretending to be snack food, or any of the other ridiculous things Ms. Dana had made us do. Did she actually design her exercises to make me look as goofy as possible in front of Derek?

I took my mind off that by thinking about Calla. What was wrong with her, anyway? Remembering that brief conversation with Duane way back when, I wondered if Glenn had said or done something mean to make her act this way. If he did, he was going to have to deal with me. I might be shy, but I would do anything for my friends!

By the time rehearsal ended, I was practically fuming. I was ready to seek out Glenn and rough him up with my bare hands, never mind that he had at least six inches and sixty pounds on me. However, the more rational part of my nature cautioned me to get the facts first. I needed to find out what he'd actually done before I decided what punishment he deserved. If Calla wasn't going to tell me, maybe Duane would.

I started looking for him. Instead, I found Nico. He was waiting for me right offstage.

"She's right, you know," he said abruptly.

"Huh?" I was still distracted by my bloodlust for Glenn. "Who's right about what?"

"Ms. Dana." He shrugged. "I know the whole 'release' thing is pretty wacked, but the general concept is right. You aren't really letting yourself go. It shows in your voice, and I guess it must show in your acting too."

I blinked, so taken aback that my anger at Glenn did an abrupt U-turn and focused on Nico instead. "Excuse me?" I snapped. "I know I asked you to help me with my singing, but I don't remember asking for an acting critique."

He frowned. "*Asked* me to help with your singing?" he retorted. "Try *begged*. And that's what I'm doing. Unless you dig deeper, you're never going to be as good as you could be."

"Whatever." I couldn't help feeling a little hurt. After all the progress I'd made, all his efforts to build me up, how could he suddenly start tearing me down? Maybe I'd been stupid to open up to him so much—to trust him. "Ms. Dana says that stuff to everyone," I pointed out icily. "And I don't hear my costar complaining." I shot a glance at Derek, my anger relaxing into a smile at the sight of him. He was across the room laughing at something Tommy had just said, looking as relaxed and handsome and generally incredible as ever.

Nico's jaw tightened. "Fine," he spat out. "I suppose this means you don't need my help anymore."

"No!" I blurted out, ripping my gaze away from Derek and turning back to Nico, the rest of my anger gone now, swallowed up by sheer panic. Nico might be getting on my nerves, but I still couldn't do this without him. "That's totally not what I meant. I just need you to focus on the singing and let me worry about the acting."

"Fine, whatever. But I still think the singing needs work." He stared at me. "You have to figure out how to let yourself go in a song. Put your whole heart and soul into it without holding back. Luckily I think I know something that might do the trick."

"Cool." My gaze was wandering back to Derek, who was still chatting with Tommy and a couple of the others. "We can work on it in study hall tomorrow."

He shook his head. "No, what I have in mind isn't going to happen during study hall. See, I want you to try singing a set with my band."

"Huh?" Once again, my attention jerked back to him. His face held the faintest hint of a smile. "What are you talking about?"

"I've mentioned my band, right? Nico and the Nasties?" He looked rather proud. "We've got a gig tomorrow night at a club downtown. You could come along and front us for a couple of songs."

I stared at him in slack-jawed, wide-eyed horror. "Sing with your punk band?" I said. "Are you kidding? No way am I doing that!"

"Come on," he urged. "It'll do you good. Trust me."

"No." I shook my head firmly. Like I said, I could be stubborn, and I could feel a *really* stubborn mood coming on right then. "Not going to happen."

He scowled at me for a moment, looking as if he wanted to say something else. Then he just shrugged. "Whatever," he said. "We'll talk about it tomorrow in study hall."

"We can talk about it all you want," I retorted, shuddering at the very thought of screaming out some obnoxious punk song in front of a bunch of jaded strangers in a downtown club. "But I'm still not going to do it."

He shrugged again. "See you in study hall."

By the time rehearsal started on Friday afternoon, Nico and I were still at a standoff about the punk-band thing. We'd spent most of study hall arguing about it, and he'd made comments about it every time he saw me all day. I wasn't giving an inch, and neither was he. In fact, he'd all but threatened to quit teaching me if I didn't go along with his crazy new plan. Nice, huh?

I steeled myself as I walked into the auditorium, expecting him to accost me and start up his haranguing again. But a quick glance around showed no sign of him. By the time Ms. Dana called for attention, he still hadn't arrived.

"All right, let's start with act two, scene five," Ms. Dana said.

"Shouldn't we wait for Nico?" I asked. Scene five was my big final song—the show-stopping title song of the show. No way was I going to be able to pull that off until my magic talisman got here, no matter how annoyed I happened to be with him at the moment.

Ms. Dana shrugged. "Nico told me earlier that he might not be able to make it today," she said. "Places, starlings!"

As the others scrambled for their marks, I swallowed hard. Nico hadn't said anything to *me* about missing rehearsal that day. What was going on?

The first part of the scene was me and Cliff having an intense confrontation. Acting opposite Derek distracted me for a while. But once I made my exit, leaving Derek onstage to finish out the scene with Tommy and some Nazi soldiers, my nerves came back full force. Where was Nico?

The rest of the scene seemed to play out in record time. Before I knew it I was step-ping back onstage for my big song. I gulped, shooting one last glance at the auditorium doors, praying to see that familiar lean form and angular face stepping through them. But no. As the music started—Ms. Dana was plunking out the melody on the piano—there was still no sign of Nico.

It's because I wouldn't go along with his stupid plan. He's doing this on purpose to punish me, I thought with a flash of irritation. *He probably thinks if he skips this rehearsal, I'll get freaked out enough to beg him to let me sing with his stupid band.*

Oh well. I would just have to call his bluff, show him that I didn't need him as much as he thought (even if I did). At least I still had my old trick to fall back on. There wasn't much real dancing in this song, so I figured I could get away with it. I closed my eyes and opened my mouth.

But the first note stuck in my throat. I coughed and tried again. No dice.

Ms. Dana stopped playing. "Maggie? Is everything okay?"

I shot her a weak smile. "Sorry," I blurted out. "Um, I think there's something in my throat. Can I skip the singing today? I don't want to, you know, damage my vocal chords or whatever."

"Of course, Maggie. We'll just move ahead to the next scene. Places!"

Whew! Crisis averted—for now. But the close call gave me a renewed sense of just how important Nico was to my musical-theater career. Not that I was ready to give in on the punk thing, of course. One bad rehearsal wasn't going to make me stark raving loony enough to agree to that. Still, I supposed it wouldn't hurt to make nice and apologize to Nico, maybe try to explain my point of view a little better . . .

"How's your throat?" Derek asked, interrupting my thoughts.

"Much better, now that you're here," I said in a sexy purr, stepping closer and wrapping my arms around him.

Okay, not really. That's what Imaginary Maggie would have said and done. Or Sally Bowles, probably. I think what I actually said was something like: "Oh! Uh, fine? I mean, it still, um, you know . . ."

He reached out and gently touched my throat with his fingers. "It's okay, sorry. Shouldn't have asked you to talk. Gotta take care of your instrument, right?"

His touch made me feel a little dizzy. But I did my best to gather my wits about me, then nodded, tilted my head, and flashed him my best smile. See? I'd show Nico that I could channel Sally when I wanted to!

"Thanks," I whispered.

We were back onstage playing out our final scene when the door opened and Nico himself walked in. I was so startled that I flubbed my line, bringing the scene to a grinding halt.

"Sorry I'm late," Nico said into the momentary silence.

"Oh, Nico, you're here." Ms. Dana turned and beamed at him. "Good. The finale is coming up, so if you could play the accompaniment, we can—"

"Wait." Nico held up his hand. "Actually, uh, I need to tell you something." He turned and shot me a cool, deliberate glance, his gaze catching mine and holding it for a second or two. Then he returned his attention to Ms. Dana. "Hate to tell you this, but I think I'm going to have to quit the show." There was a collective gasp at that. It was hard to imagine a Thespians show without Nico. "Don't worry," he went on before anyone could respond. "I already talked to Ella DiMarco and Mike Nelson, and they're willing to step in and take over for me. Ella is an awesome musician; she'll be able to pick up the piano accompaniment in no time, and she can totally handle directing the band for the show too, probably better than I can. And Mike will take care of the sound-mixing and other behind-the-scenes stuff I usually do. I'll show him what you need so there won't be any snags during the transition."

"Nico, this is such a surprise!" Ms. Dana exclaimed, looking startled. "Are you sure about this?"

"No way, dude!" Duane put in. "You can't quit. We need you!"

Rosalie nodded. "It wouldn't be the same without you!"

"First Mr. Fayne, and now you? You can't do this to us, Nico!" Jenna added plaintively.

Part of me was a little surprised that they all sounded so genuinely distressed. True, Nico did a lot for the Thespians. But it sounded as if he'd lined up competent replacements already, so why did the others care that much? It wasn't as if any of them were his best buddies or anything.

But most of me was distracted by other, much more pressing matters. That glance at me had been as easy to read as a large-print book. I'd called his bluff, and now he was calling mine. What would happen if he actually went through with this? I could almost see the headline in the school paper now:

THEATER REVIEW: TONE-DEAF TANNERY MANGLES MUSICAL

COSTARS CAN'T SAVE AUDIENCE FROM STAR'S SCARY "SINGING"

"No!" I blurted out desperately, banishing the horrible fantasy from my mind. "He's just kidding, you guys."

"What?" Ms. Dana blinked at me, looking confused.

"Tell them, Nico." I glared at him. "He, uh, it's, um, an . . . an acting exercise. I sort of dared him to do it—I thought it would, you know, shake us all out of our comfort zones and give new urgency to our roles. Or something. Anyway it's all my fault, and I'm sorry. I'll do anything you want to make it up to you guys. *Anything*." I widened my eyes at Nico significantly, hoping he got the message. He'd won. I gave in. I'd even do his stupid punk song, just as long as he didn't abandon me like this.

"Interesting!" Predictably enough, Ms. Dana looked intrigued by my lame acting-exercise excuse.

But the others still seemed kind of confused. "Nico?" Duane said, turning to stare at him.

There was what felt like a very long moment of silence. I'm talking decades long. Finally, Nico shrugged and gave his wry little half smile.

"Yeah, she's right," he said. "Sorry, you guys. Guess it was a pretty lame joke. I tried to tell her you wouldn't appreciate it, but you know Maggie when she gets an idea in her head . . ."

The others were so relieved that they didn't even seem mad, though Tommy did march over and give him a sound punch in the arm. Meanwhile all I could do was slump down on a handy chair, shaking with a combination of relief and dread. What had I just gotten myself into?

Fifteen

"I hate you, you know," I told Nico, clutching the microphone he'd just handed me.

He glanced up from plugging an amp into the ratty-looking power strip on the ratty-looking wooden stage in the ratty music club and smiled. "I know," he said. "But this is for your own good. Trust me."

I wasn't too sure I should. What good could come of this ridiculous experiment? It was like one of Ms. Dana's wacky exercises, only worse. This time I wouldn't just be making a fool of myself in front of my fellow actors, who were also making fools of themselves. This was public. Well, some scary, overly pierced and tattooed version of the public, anyway. I peered around the club. It wasn't much bigger than the music room at school, though it was much dingier and more poorly lit. The walls were scrawled with graffiti, some of it shockingly crude. A bar stood against one end of the room, barely visible behind throngs of patrons, who seemed to range from fairly conventional-looking frat boy types to gloomy goths to old-school punks complete with mohawks and safety pins. I was standing on the stage at the opposite end of the room along with Nico and the rest of the Nasties. The stage itself was a rickety wooden platform, maybe ten feet square and three feet high. It was crammed with amps and speakers, their accompanying wiring snaking out and threatening to trip me at every step.

Shooting a glance at Nico's rather fright-ening and exotic-looking bandmates, who were setting up their instruments, I won-dered what they thought of this situation. On the ride over Nico had taught me the lyrics and melody for the song I was sup-posed to sing with them, but I'd been too nervous to retain much of it.

"Listen, I seriously don't know if I can do this," I hissed at him, watching out of the corner of my eye as one of his bandmates shrugged off his jacket to reveal a giant tattoo of a nuclear mushroom cloud across his shoulder blades. Or maybe it was just supposed to be a mushroom. I certainly wasn't about to strike up a conversation with the guy to find out. "I don't even remember the whole song."

Finishing with the amp, Nico straightened up and looked at me. He took back the microphone and then stepped over to place it into the metal stand at the front of the stage. Even through my terror and annoyance I had to admit he looked pretty hot. I was used to seeing him as just regular old Nico, slightly scruffy in his black jeans and T-shirts. But tonight he actually looked like a rock star. His dark eyes were lined with charcoal, his hair was awesomely crazy, and his long, lean legs were encased in form-fitting leather pants.

"Don't sweat the small stuff," he told me calmly when he turned back toward me. "Lyrics and melody don't matter that much in punk."

"What?" I blinked at him, not sure I'd heard him right. It was kind of loud in there, between the thuds and clangs of the equipment setup, the blaring radio by the bar, and the rather raucous clientele.

He shrugged. "It's all about the attitude. If you can pull that off, you're golden."

"But what if I *can't* pull it off?" I asked. Unfortunately, at that moment, the band's bass player let out an ear-shattering burst that I guess was supposed to be a chord. There was an immediate loud whine of feedback from the speakers, and the audience jeered lustily.

"Get it together, man!" a tough-looking girl with green hair shouted from the audience, tossing a nacho at the bass player. "We want some music!"

"Music? What's that, sweetheart?" the bass player taunted in return, kicking the nacho back toward her.

Most of the audience was now crowding up around the stage, making me feel a bit claustrophobic. It didn't help that several of the guys were staring me up and down in an uncomfortable way. I tugged at the hem of my shirt, feeling self-conscious about what I was wearing. Nico had told me I'd be fine in jeans and a black T. But now that I was here, dressed in my Old Navy jeans and my cropped V-neck from the Gap, I felt a little like a toy poodle dropped suddenly into a gang of rottweilers.

I turned around, trying not to think about all those guys now staring at my butt, and followed Nico toward the back of the stage. I might be mad at him for making me do this, but he was still my only beacon of familiarity in this sea of scary weirdness.

"Seriously," I told him, my voice shaking a little. "I'm so nervous I feel like I might throw up."

"This crowd might like that," Nico said with a half smile.

One of the other band members, a tall guy with wild red dreadlocks and an Australian accent, overheard us. "Yeah, babe," he said with a grin. "Chick vomit is hot!"

I shuddered as Nico laughed. Feeling tears welling up in my eyes, I turned away, not wanting them to see how upset I was. They seemed to think this was all a big joke. That *I* was a big joke.

A second later I felt a hand on my shoulder. "Hey. Chill, Maggie, okay?" Nico murmured in my ear, sounding much more sympathetic than he had a second ago. "You'll be okay. I wouldn't have brought you if I didn't believe you could handle this. Seriously. I wouldn't do that to you."

I blinked away my tears and glanced

at him. "How would you know what I can handle?"

He shrugged. "Maybe I know you better than you think." There was another sudden deafening chord, and he glanced over his shoulder. "Looks like we're just about ready. I'll do the first song, and then yours is next, okay?"

"No!" I blurted out, but my protest was lost in a sudden explosion of sound as the drummer started playing and the bass and guitar players immediately joined in. The music, if you could call it that, was so loud that it seemed to fill my entire body, snake through my veins, and pour into my bones, making me sort of pulse from the inside out. I'd never felt anything like it.

I backed off to the side of the stage—but not too far. It was open on three sides, and I had the same feeling I'd had sometimes as a little kid when I'd woken up in the middle of the night and huddled in the center of my bed, arms and legs clutched tight against my body, fearing that something might grab at me out of the sea of darkness surrounding me.

Nico strode to the front of the stage and grabbed the microphone stand. "Okay, people!" he shouted aggressively into the mic as the rest of the band paused. "Let's do this thing!"

The band immediately swung into a driving, fast-paced song with a throbbing bass line and cacophonous guitar. In spite of myself, I felt my head nodding in time with the beat the drummer was banging out. It was like the music was physically grabbing me and shaking me. The volume increased even more, making it hard to think.

Nico howled out the opening lyrics—something about pain—at the top of his lungs, his voice raspy and hard. It was difficult to believe this was the same guy I'd heard croon out "My Favorite Things" like Julie Andrews or imitate a saucy Kit Kat Girl on many other occasions. It was kind of fascinating. I'd always thought of myself as much more complicated than most people probably saw me. I wasn't just shy good-girl actress Maggie Tannery—I was also all the Maggies I'd ever invented inside my head. I'd known that Nico wasn't exactly one-dimensional either, what with the punk rock/theater/opera camp thing. But this was really the first time I was seeing that so clearly in person.

The song ended as abruptly as it had begun, with a raucous final thrash of drums and a squeal from the guitar. "Thank you!" Nico shouted as the audience wailed out its approval. "And now, a special treat—we've got a guest singer for our next number. Say hello to the very talented, very sexy Maggie Tannery!"

The crowd cheered and I felt my face go red again. This was it. I wanted to run screaming for the exit, but that would mean pushing my way through a bunch of intimidating and possibly hostile punks to get there. I was trapped.

Nico stepped over and held out his hand. "Come on," he said, though I could only tell that by reading his lips. The din was deafening.

I took his hand and allowed him to pull me forward. "I can't do this," I whimpered, though I couldn't even hear it myself.

Besides, Nico had already stepped back. He lifted one hand, and the noise subsided slightly.

"One, two, three, four!" he shouted, and with that the band launched into another song that sounded an awful lot like the first.

The music enveloped me again, and for a second I couldn't move. The crowd was still yelling. If I didn't start singing soon, they'd probably start throwing nachos at me. Or worse.

Leaning a little closer to the microphone, I fished for the opening line. "I don't care, uh, care what you think," I squeaked out. Even with the microphone on, I could hardly hear myself over the band. And what I could hear sounded pretty pathetic.

The audience thought so too. A few people booed. Others were glaring at me. For a second I was ready to run off the stage and hide under the pile of guitar cases in the alley out back.

Then there was a rush of movement behind me. A second later Nico was there, his shoulder touching mine as he leaned down to sing into my microphone.

"I don't care what you think!" he sang. "You drive me straight to drink."

I shot him a grateful look. He looked back at me, mouthing the words "sing with me."

I gulped, still not sure I could do this. Still, what did I have to lose at this point? I watched Nico out of the corner of my eye, taking comfort in his familiar presence.

Then I opened my mouth and joined in on the next line: "I don't care what you say, you suck the life out of every day."

At first my voice was still tentative, barely audible above Nico and the band. But when we reached the chorus, which basically went "I don't care" over and over about fifteen times, Nico reached over and grabbed me, squeezing me around the shoulders.

That gave me the extra little bit of courage I needed. "I don't care! I don't care!" I yelled into the mic, feeling a little goofy but trying not to worry about it. "I don't give a damn!"

On the next verse I let myself out a notch, putting a little growl into the lines and then yelling out the chorus at the top of my lungs. After a while Nico stepped back a bit, only singing backup on the chorus and letting me handle the rest.

And you know what? Once I got past the sheer gut-clenching terror, it was actually sort of . . . fun? Maybe that was too strong a word. Ms. Dana might have called it "freeing." Nobody was going to notice if I blew a note or messed up the words. Nobody would care. *I* didn't care.

On the next chorus I belted out my "I

don't care's" with abandon. And when the last verse started, even though I'd forgotten most of the lyrics, I went for it anyway. Whenever I couldn't remember the words, I either made some up or just let out a scream instead.

And the audience loved it! By the end of the song they were jumping up and down and shouting for more. I took a bow, my face bright red—not that anyone could tell in the dim light of the club—but with a big smile.

"Well?" Nico leaned toward me, his cheek actually touching mine as he whispered directly into my ear. "Want to try another one?"

I took a deep breath. "Yeah," I said, turning toward him. His face was so close I could feel his breath mingle with mine. "I think I will."

"Cool." He smiled at me for a second, then turned away to signal to the band. A moment later they started another number. The opening chords sounded sort of familiar, though for a second I couldn't place the song.

Then I laughed out loud as I finally recognized it. It was a punked-out, stripped-down version of "Mein Herr"! Now that I thought about it, that song did have kind of a punk vibe to it—leave it to Nico to notice!

I was still laughing as I started to sing. Nico stayed up there with me, occasionally joining in but mostly letting me do it myself. And I have to admit, I had a great time attacking the familiar lyrics, giving the song a little extra edge. I had a feeling Ms. Dana might be surprised by how I sounded on it at our next rehearsal!

After that Nico took over again, though I stuck around and contributed some impromptu backup vocals, mostly just making up whatever words and notes I wanted. It was weird and still kind of scary, but exhilarating at the same time. By the end of the show I was back to screaming out crazy made-up punk lyrics at the top of my lungs, having kind of almost a good time.

"Thank you, good-night!" Nico shouted after the last song, saluting the crowd. Then he turned to me and grabbed me, wrapping me in a big hug. "Awesome job, Maggie. I knew you had it in you!" he cried into my ear.

I hugged him back, still caught up in the excitement of what I'd just done. He'd been right. I *did* have it in me. Who knew? Now that this was over and I'd survived, I was grateful to him for making me do it. After this, Sally Bowles was going to be a snap!

"Yo, get a room!" someone yelled from nearby. Looking up over Nico's shoulder, I saw his bandmates grinning at us.

"Shoulda known," the Australian guy said with a smirk. "Leave it to Vasquez to bring in his own personal Yoko."

Nico dropped his arms and stepped back, shooting his bandmates an irritated look. "Grow up," he muttered at them. Glancing back at me without quite meeting my eye, he added, "I'd better go help the guys pack up."

"Okay," I said, though he was already hurrying away. I spent the next few minutes perched on a speaker, wondering why things so often seemed to end up weird and awkward between us.

Sixteen

"Maggie! Hi."

I spun around and almost tripped over my own feet. Naturally, it was Derek.

"Um . . ." I searched my brain for the correct response.

Say hi, doofus, my brain ordered with disdain.

"Um . . . ," my mouth responded again.

Why do I even try? You're hopeless, my brain muttered, throwing up its hands. Uh, or its synapses. Or whatever.

Meanwhile Derek was still smiling down at me, seemingly unaware of the epic battle raging inside my head. "So how was your weekend?" he asked. "Do anything fun?"

"Yah," I blurted out. "Uh, I mean, no. Not

really. What about—what did you do?"

It was Monday morning, and I'd spent the entire weekend recovering from my punk debut. I couldn't seem to stop thinking about how I'd felt up there, screaming my lungs out and not caring what anyone thought. Not that I was about to share such thoughts with Derek, even if I could manage to speak clearly enough to do so. For one thing, he didn't seem like the kind of guy who would appreciate the whole punk scene. Besides, I would have felt oddly disloyal telling him I'd done something like that with another guy, even if it was only Nico. I definitely didn't want to send him any wrong signals.

"Not a whole lot." Derek shrugged. "Couple of parties, the usual. Mostly worked on my history paper and practiced my lines. If I screw up scene nine one more time, Ms. Dana will kill me!"

"N-no," I stammered. "She'll make you pretend to be . . . to be . . ." I got stuck and floundered helplessly for a moment.

He chuckled. "She'll make me pretend to be a suitcase full of Nazi secrets?" he joked. "Or were you going to say she'll want me to imagine I'm a pineapple? It's hard to guess what she'll come up with, isn't it?"

"Yeah," I said with relief. Silly me! What had prompted me to attempt a witty remark when I could barely manage to exchange pleasantries? Maybe that punk act had made me a little braver than I could handle.

Derek checked his watch, then reached over and gave me a friendly tap on the shoulder. "Oops, gotta go. See you at rehearsal."

"See you." As long as I stuck to words of one syllable, I seemed to mostly do okay.

As he disappeared into the pre-homeroom crowds, Calla stepped forward. I hadn't even noticed her standing nearby, even though I'd gone that way looking for her at her locker. "Well, that was smooth," she said, reaching for her locker door.

I collapsed against the row of lockers, allowing the cool metal to bring me back to my senses. "Yeah, yeah, I know," I moaned. "What is it with me, anyway? Derek and I have been totally clicking onstage. So why can't I get it together when we're not acting?"

She shrugged. "Mystery of the universe, babe," she said. "Maybe you should've invited him to see your big punk debut on Friday." She grinned at me. "Still can't believe you didn't invite me and Duane to that. Well, at least me. I can understand why you wouldn't want Duane there. He'd probably want to jump up onstage and take over. Totally embarrassing, right?"

I flashed from the heady feeling of letting loose onstage to that awkward hug with Nico. "Yeah, right," I said. "But listen, that reminds me. I've been meaning to ask you about something. Are you having any trouble with Glenn? You know—in the show?"

She bent down and rummaged loudly through the lower shelf of her locker. "I don't know what you mean." Her voice coming from inside the locker sounded tinny and echoey. "No trouble other than the usual—you know, Glenn being Glenn. We always knew he was a dork. We can't all have the chemistry you and Loverboy do onstage." With that she emerged from the locker and glanced at me. "Listen, that gives me a great idea. You know what you were just saying about not being able to talk to Derek when you're not acting?"

"Yeah?" I wanted to stop her, to return to our previous topic. But when Calla gets going, she's kind of like a freight train.

Your only choices are to hop on board or get run over.

"I have a great idea. Why don't we write you out a script? You know—for talking to Dreamboy in real life." She grinned, seeming pleased with herself. "See, you're an actress, right? As long as you have your lines memorized, you can do anything. Maybe if you start off like that, it'll get you over the hump." She smirked. "So to speak."

"A script to talk to Derek?" I said, still a little distracted by thinking about her and Glenn. "Um, I don't know . . ."

She flung her arm around my shoulders with such enthusiasm that it nearly knocked me off my feet. "I do," she said confidently. "This will work. I guarantee it."

On Wednesday morning, I was forced—er, able—to put Calla's plan into motion. She'd come over after rehearsal on Tuesday to help me write the script. We'd had an awesome rehearsal, so I was in a good mood. Derek and I had run our final two scenes of the show a couple of times, and I don't think it was my imagination—we'd thrown off some serious sparks. Ms. Dana seemed thrilled with my performance, and especially with the way I'd attacked the title song.

"Finally!" she'd said gleefully. "You've discovered the essence of Sally! Well done, Maggie."

I'd just smiled and thanked her, then shot a glance at Nico. He'd grinned and winked.

So anyway, I'd been too high on life to protest very hard against Calla's goofy plan and had ended up just sort of going along with it as she wrote out a whole script for me. And now here I was, my lines memorized like the good little actress I was, wondering if I was really going to go through with this. I was still wondering when I ran into Nico outside the auditorium.

"Maggie!" he said with a smile. "Hey, didn't get to talk to you after rehearsal yesterday. How about what Ms. Dana said to you? Told you that punk gig would do the trick, huh?"

"Uh, yeah." I shot a nervous look around me. I had too many other things on my mind just then to focus on chitchat with Nico. "Listen, can we talk about that later? I have to, uh, be somewhere."

"Oh." Nico shrugged. "Sure. Catch you later."

I hurried off down the hall, rounding the next corner so fast that I almost ran smack into Derek himself. "Eep!" I squeaked out. "Urp," I added as Derek turned and spotted me.

Without waiting for him to say a word, I took a deep breath and launched into Calla's script. What did I have to lose? Trying the lines she'd written for me couldn't possibly make me sound like any more of an idiot than I was likely to manage on my own . . . could it?

The next few minutes went something like this:

ME: Hi, Derek! What's up?

DEREK: Hey, Maggie. Not much. What's up with you?

ME: Just the usual. Ready for that trig quiz today?

WHAT DEREK WAS SUPPOSED TO SAY: Ready as I'll ever be!

WHAT DEREK ACTUALLY SAID: Wait, trig quiz? What trig quiz?

ME, *still on script*: Yeah, me too. Horvath's quizzes are killer, aren't they?

WDWSTS: I know, right?

WDAS, *sounding panicky*: Are you serious? Do we really have a quiz today? What's it going to cover?

ME, *realizing this is off the rails but not sure how to switch gears now*: So Calla and Duane and I were talking about the cast party after the show. I know it's a little early, since we still have like two weeks to go until opening night. But since it's already getting warm out, we were thinking pool party at Bethany's house. What do you think?

WSWSTS: Awesome. I'll dig out my trunks and water wings.

WDAS: Hang on, back up. About this quiz—

ME: Yeah, I think it'll be fun. We always have a blast at our cast parties.

WDWSTS: Cool. I love a good party.

WDAS, *frantic*: Maggie, what's with you? Was the quiz thing a joke or something? Because I seriously don't get it.

ME, *increasingly desperate, sort of like*

*someone trying to steer a car with no
brakes. Or steering wheel. And with
snow completely covering the windshield:* Me too. And nobody parties
like a bunch of Thespians who just
finished a show!

By now Derek was staring at me as if I
had three heads. And no wonder.

"S-sorry," I blurted out, inwardly curs-
ing Calla while finally yanking myself off-
script through sheer force of embarrassment.
"Um, guess I got, you know, distracted or
something. Um, the quiz is . . . it's on the
stuff we did yesterday. I think it's chapter
sixteen."

"Oh, man." Derek yanked his backpack higher on his shoulder, looking grim.
"Listen, I'll talk to you later, okay? I've got
some serious cramming to do before second
period."

"Okay. Bye," I said to his departing
back, as usual feeling like the world's biggest spaz. Yeah, way to impress him with
my wit and charm.

Oh well. At least we had rehearsals . . .

Seventeen

"Sorry, Mags," Calla said again. We were sitting in our third-period English class waiting for the teacher to arrive. I'd just filled her in on that morning's disaster with Derek. "I really thought the script thing would work."

"I know you did."

My irritation with her had faded quickly once I'd had a moment to recover. After all, she'd meant well—she always did. Who else would have put up with all my long-distance mooning over Derek all these years, let alone tried to help me win him now? Only a true friend.

And I was determined to be a true friend to her in return. Once again, I'd allowed other issues to crowd her recent odd behavior out of my mind for a while. But no more. I was getting to the bottom of it—today.

"Listen, enough about me," I said. "Let's talk about you. I can't help noticing you've been having some trouble onstage lately. Is acting with ghastly Glenn just throwing you off your game, or is something else going on?"

"Boys don't throw me off my game, darling," she said airily. "I throw them off theirs."

"Stop," I cut her off sternly. "Don't pull that with me, Calla. I'm an actress too, remember? I can tell you're not being straight with me."

For a second she looked annoyed. Then she sighed and her face went sort of sad. "Okay, you're right," she said just as the teacher finally walked in. "I'll tell you later. Promise."

"Later" turned out to be that afternoon right after school. We had the day off from rehearsal, so Calla offered me a ride home. Once we were in the car, I turned to her.

"Okay, let's hear it," I said.

She didn't have to ask me what I meant.

Putting the car into gear, she peeled out of the student parking lot.

"It's totally stupid," she said, staring straight ahead through the fly-specked windshield. "That's why I haven't said anything."

I leaned closer. "Is it Glenn?" I asked. "Did he say something obnoxious? Is he feeling you up during your dance scenes or something? Or is he just making like he's the only one in the world who knows anything about acting?"

"No, nothing like that. Well, yeah, on the last part, but that's just Glenn. No biggie." She shrugged and squealed to a halt at a stop sign before shooting me a glance. "And it's not even about Glenn, not really. It's more about me."

"I don't understand." That was an understatement. Calla, normally the most supremely self-confident person I knew, was suddenly sounding as conflicted and tentative as, well, me.

She tilted her head back and blew out a sigh in the direction of the car roof. This was slightly unnerving, given that she'd just peeled out from the stop sign and was careening down Schoolhouse Road. But I kept quiet about that.

"It's just, I don't know," she said, finally returning her gaze to the road. "At first I was psyched about playing Fraulein Schneider. It's a big part, and the songs are cool. And I can really get into the tragic torn-apart-by-Nazis love story thing, you know?"

"The role is definitely in your wheel-house," I agreed. "So what's the problem?"

"Getting to that." She spun the wheel, lurching around the corner on two tires. At least it felt that way. "The thing is, Glenn and I have to act like we're, you know, in love. Naturally, even that kind of huge challenge is no problem for my immense talent." She patted her hair, for a moment looking and sounding like her normal self.

"But?" I prompted.

She sighed and shot me a glance before returning her eyes to the road. "But the thing is, I think it's a little harder for Glenn. Especially when we have to, you know, touch. Or dance. Or anything where he's reminded I'm not some ninety-pound cheerleader type." She shook her head. "I saw it in his face the first time he was supposed to put his arms around me."

"Has he said anything to you?" I asked. "You know, um, about your . . . your size?"

She shrugged so expressively that the car zigzagged in an alarming manner, almost taking out a mailbox. "He doesn't have to. He's not nearly as good an actor as he thinks he is."

"Oh!" I had to admit it, I was too surprised to say anything else for a moment. This was a new development indeed. Calla had always been overweight. She'd also always been forthright about that, usually making the jokes before anyone else could. Call me dense, but it had never occurred to me that she could actually be insecure about it.

"Never mind," Calla muttered. "Like I said, it's no big deal."

"No, it's okay," I said quickly. "I'm here if you want to, you know, talk about it. Or whatever." I wasn't sure what else to say. Any commiseration would likely come out sounding fake—Calla knew as well as anyone that I'd been effortlessly slim my whole life.

She shot me a look, clearly thinking along the same lines. "Thanks, but no thanks. You can't possibly understand what it's like."

That stung a little. "So what if I can't?"

I responded. "That doesn't mean I don't want to help. I mean, you can't understand how it is to be shy, but you've always tried to help me with that."

"Whatever." She removed both hands from the wheel and waved them around as if shooing away a fly. "Let's just drop it, okay?"

I frowned and leaned back against the vinyl seat, feeling frustrated. How was I supposed to help Calla with her problem if she wouldn't even let me try?

Another day, another great rehearsal with Derek. The show was really coming together by now. The props, scenery, and costume people had been working like crazy. The Kit Kat Klub now consisted of actual tables and chairs, Duane had a real old-fashioned brass-topped cane to use in some of his dances, and Derek got to play his smuggling scenes with a classy-looking old leather briefcase borrowed from someone's grandfather. We weren't rehearsing in our full costumes and makeup, of course—that would wait until next week's dress rehearsal. But I *was* wearing my high-heeled dance shoes, wanting to get as much practice in them as possible so I wouldn't trip over my own feet when I tried to dance in the show. And Derek was practicing wearing a hat at all times so he'd look smooth and natural putting it on and taking it off. The exotic foot- and headwear somehow seemed to give our scenes a little extra oomph.

We finished that day's rehearsal with a run-through of act one, scene five, which ended with my duet with Derek, "Perfectly Marvelous." We were supposed to get closer and closer through the last part of the song, until we were in each other's arms as the lights went out. Let me tell you, I never got tired of rehearsing that particular moment!

"And . . . hold!" Ms. Dana cried as we held the pose for a beat and then started to straighten up. "No, don't move yet! Remember, you two need to stay perfectly still until the stage goes dark."

"Sorry." Derek winked at me. "Come on, Sally. We'd better practice that again to show her we can do it." He grabbed me, squeezing me tight for a long moment. I stared up at him, breathless. He returned the stare, back in Cliff mode, his eyes adoring. After a few seconds the rest of the cast started to hoot and holler playfully as they watched us.

"All right, that's enough." Ms. Dana sounded amused. "I'm convinced."

"Are you sure?" Derek called without taking his eyes off me.

"Come on, dude!" Tommy called back. "If you want to cuddle with your costar, do it on your own time. The rest of us are ready to get out of here!"

That made us both laugh. We parted and stepped back.

"Nice job, everyone," Ms. Dana said. "We'll do it again tomorrow. Don't forget, after that it's only a week until opening night!"

"Wow, opening night," Derek commented as the two of us headed for the steps leading off the stage. "Hard to believe!"

I was still mostly in Sally mode, so I was actually able to respond coherently. "I know. Part of me feels totally ready and excited, but another part wishes we had, like, three more years of rehearsal to get ready." Oh, if only he knew how true that really was!

He chuckled. "I hear you! By the way, speaking of being ready for things, I almost forgot—thanks for the heads-up on that trig quiz yesterday. I actually managed to pull off a B." He laughed and raked a hand through his hair. "Of course, I have no idea what Mr. Michaels talked about in my first-period English class."

"Oh." I thought that was an awfully nice way for him to describe our weird conversation yesterday. "Um, you're welcome."

He smiled down at me. "Maybe I'll have to thank you by taking you out to a movie or something sometime. What do you say?"

"Oh!" That seemed to be my favorite word today. My mind raced, trying to process what my ears had just delivered to it. Was I finally going crazy for real, slipping irretrievably into my own fantasies? Or had the *real* Derek just asked the *real* me out on a *real* date?

"Hey!" Nico hurried up at that moment, interrupting my racing thoughts. "Good rehearsal, guys. You both looked great up there."

"Thanks, dude." Derek held out a hand for one of those slap/shake things that guys are always doing.

Nico obliged, though it looked a little funny. He's not really the slap/shake kind of guy.

"Listen, can I borrow Maggie for a sec?" he asked Derek.

No! No! my mind shouted frantically. *Say no, Derek!*

"Sure," Derek said easily. "My ride's waiting for my anyway." He reached out and squeezed my upper arm. "We'll talk tomorrow, Maggie."

With that, he was gone. I stared after him, wondering if I really had imagined the whole date thing.

Nico didn't seem to notice my state of distraction. "Hey, I wanted to see if you could make it to my next gig tomorrow night," he said. "We're playing at the same club."

"Why? I thought you were already happy with my, like, big punk breakthrough or whatever."

He chuckled. "Yeah, don't worry. You don't have to sing this time. I just thought you might want to hear this new song I just wrote for the band. It's . . . it's pretty cool, if I do say so myself."

By now coming out of my Derek-induced haze, I noticed that Nico had kind of an odd expression on his face. I wasn't sure what that was about, but I figured if he really wanted me to come to his show, it was the least I could do after all his help.

Besides, it might be kind of fun, especially if Calla and Duane wanted to tag along—I knew Duane especially would get a kick out of the club. I only wished I had the guts to invite Derek. Somehow, though, I suspected he already had plans for Friday night, and they probably didn't include punk music or graffiti-splattered clubs.

"Sure," I told Nico. "Sounds cool. I'll be there."

"You were right, Mags." Duane stared around the punk club. "This place is da bomb!"

Calla rolled her eyes at him. "'Da bomb'?" she mimicked. "What is this, 1995?"

"You know time stands still whenever I'm with you, babe," he drawled, reaching out and grabbing her around the waist with both arms. She squealed and pushed him away, leading to a silly slapping-and-wrestling match.

It was a familiar scene, one I'd seen played out a million times. But tonight I watched them goof around together with new eyes. Duane was way skinnier than Glenn, and Calla didn't seem self-conscious about that at all. So why was she letting her love scenes with Glenn bother her so much?

I had to admit I didn't quite get it.

Just then Nico and his bandmates appeared, distracting me from such thoughts. Calla spotted them too.

"Whoo-hoo!" she shouted, cupping her hands around her mouth. "Check out the rock star!"

Nico glanced over. He spotted me first and smiled. Then he noticed Calla and Duane and raised an eyebrow in surprise. They were both waving at him by now, and he lifted one hand in return before turning away to help one of the others lift an amp onto the stage.

"Kinda fun to see Mr. Cool in his element, huh?" Duane commented.

"Yeah." Calla grinned. "I'm surprised he even acknowledged that he knew a bunch of dorks like us."

"He probably figured everyone assumes we're just crazy fans." Duane raised his arms over his head and let out a "Whoo hoo! Rock and roll!" A few of the other patrons glanced toward him in surprise.

I smiled weakly, hoping we weren't embarrassing Nico. But I didn't worry about it too much. Nico didn't seem to let much bother him; I doubted a few yells from Duane and Calla would throw him off his game.

A few minutes later the Nasties started their set. They kicked if off with the "I Don't Care" song I'd sung with them before, and then continued with a few others I vaguely recognized. Duane and Calla were grooving to the driving punk beat, even doing some crazy fast-paced swing dancing together at one point, with Duane's long arms and legs flying so wildly that even the scariest-looking punks backed away and kept a wary eye on him. I watched from a safe distance, wishing Calla could figure out how to let go and enjoy herself with Glenn onstage the way she was doing with Duane now.

Then the current song ended and Nico lifted the microphone. "And now we're going to do a new song," he said. "I call it 'Actress.'"

"Oh, cool," Calla exclaimed breathlessly, stepping back over to me. "This one must be about me."

The band launched into the song. It was a bit slower paced than most of the others, and Nico's voice rang out clearly, with only a hint of his usual punk roughness.

"I know a girl, a talented girl," he sang,

his eyes scanning the crowd. "Her long yellow hair sets my heart aswirl."

"Hmm," Calla said into my ear. "Maybe it's not about me after all."

I blushed as Nico turned and found me, his eyes locking onto mine. "She's an actress, wants to hide what she feels," he sang. "But I see through her act to the part that's real . . ."

My head spun. Was this why he'd been so eager for me to come tonight? To have me hear this? It was just too unexpected, too weird . . . What if I'd summoned up the guts to invite Derek along after all? Talk about embarrassing!

"No," I blurted out, unable to process it all. "I . . . this is too . . . I've got to go!"

Without waiting for a response from my friends, I turned and pushed my way blindly out of the club.

By the time I arrived at home, I regretted my impulsive departure. What was the huge deal? So Nico had a crush on me just as Calla had said all along—awkward, yes, but not worthy of such drama. If anything, I should be flattered that he cared enough to write a song about me. How hard would it have been to sit through it, then let him down easy in private after the show? As it was, though, I'd pretty much humiliated him in front of his bandmates and an entire clubful of people. I had to apologize, to try to explain. . . .

He didn't pick up his cell phone for the rest of that night or any of the eleven or twelve times I tried calling him on Saturday morning. I was frantic by then—was he avoiding me? Had I ruined things between us for good? I couldn't stand the thought. Sure, I'd needed to let him know in no uncertain terms that I wasn't interested in him in *that* way. But I was heartbroken at the thought of losing him as a friend. I'd really come to count on him lately. I mean, sure, he had his oddball qualities. I'd always known that. But now I knew he had a sweet side too. He really listened to me, he'd helped me even when I didn't think I needed it, and he knew how to make me laugh. All those things suddenly seemed superprecious and superimportant. Maybe even more important than the additional fact that I really needed to have him around if I hoped to make it through next weekend's performances without making a total fool of myself . . .

By lunchtime I still hadn't reached him on the phone. Finally I had to face facts. There were really just two possibilities here: (a) Nico's phone was broken; or (b) he was avoiding me.

Okay, so I tried to convince myself there were a few other options, like alien invasion or terrorists taking over the punk club after I'd left. But those attempts were halfhearted at best. No, it was pretty obvious that the most likely answer was that he didn't want to talk to me. And after my behavior, who could blame him? Friends didn't treat friends that way. At least, they weren't supposed to. I needed to find him and force him to let me apologize in person.

Luckily, I knew just where he was likely to be. A few minutes later I was walking into the Thornton Diner. As usual for a Saturday afternoon, the place was packed. The jukebox was playing some old song from the fifties, and the buzz of laughter and conversation bounced off the shiny silver walls. Glancing around, I recognized at least a dozen faces from school. Like I said, our town didn't have a whole lot of options when it came to going out.

But there was no sign of Nico. When I

asked the girl at the hostess desk about him, she shrugged.

"He's not in today," she said, popping her gum. "Called in sick."

"Oh. Thanks." I backed away, wondering uneasily if I had anything to do with Nico's absence.

Suddenly the cheerful, noisy, crowded diner seemed stifling. I hurried for the door, gasping for breath, and pushed through it. I skidded to stop as I almost crashed into someone just coming up the concrete steps.

"Sorry!" I blurted out.

"Maggie?"

"Derek!" I gasped. Yeah. It was him. What were the odds? "Um, I . . ." As usual, I couldn't seem to string three words together in a coherent sentence. This time, however, it was only partly due to Derek's magnificence. I was still distracted by the whole Nico situation.

Derek looked concerned. "Hey, are you okay?" he asked. "You look kind of upset."

"I am," I said before I could stop myself. "I mean, I—"

"Want to go inside and talk about it?" He put a hand on my arm as if to steer me back into the diner.

"No!" I blurted out. "Um, I mean, thanks. I don't want to go in there, though—too, um, noisy."

"I hear you. Come on."

He kept his hand on my arm, but this time turned and steered me down the steps and across the street to the town park, a large, mostly wooded area that covered about fifteen acres between the public golf course and the middle school sports fields. Before I knew it, the two of us were sitting on a bench with no one in sight but a squirrel or two.

"There," Derek said, turning to face me with a smile. "Now how can I help you feel better? I hate seeing you upset."

"Oh." I wasn't sure what to say to that. My mind had been so focused on the Nico thing for the past fifteen hours or so that it was having trouble keeping up with this latest development. "Um, it's not that big a deal. I just had a . . . a fight with Nico. An argument, um, about, well, it doesn't matter. See, he's been helping me with my singing and stuff, and I really don't want him mad at me so close to the show . . ."

"Bummer." Derek put a hand on my knee. I stared at it, as surprised to see it there as if it had been a grenade or a tentacle or something. "But listen, I'm sure Nico will get over it. No guy could stay mad at you for long."

I gulped. He was smiling at me in a weird sort of way. Before I could process what that smile might mean, he put his other arm around me and pulled me closer. A second later, we were kissing. My head spun. Was this really happening?

Don't ask stupid questions, my lips scolded my brain. *Just go with it.*

So that's exactly what I did. My lips melded with his. My hands pressed against his chest, that strong, muscular chest I'd dreamed about for so long . . .

"Oh!" I gasped out when we finally came up for air. "Wow. I, um, that was . . . that was nice."

"Yeah," he murmured, his hand tracing patterns up and down my back. "I'm really glad I ran into you today, Maggie. I've been wanting to, you know, get together with you outside of rehearsal. You just always seem so busy."

Busy? Okay, if that's what he wanted to call it, I wasn't going to argue.

"I'm glad too," I said.

He smiled and tucked a strand of my

hair behind my ear, then traced my cheek-bone with one finger, making me shudder. Then his face moved toward mine again. I let my eyes flutter shut and my lips flutter open as they found his. My hands snaked around his waist, and his clutched at my back. For a moment Nico's scowling face danced through my mind and I felt a flash of guilt. But I pushed that aside. Derek was right. If Nico was a true friend, we would work through it . . . later.

Eighteen

"Nicely done, Derek and Maggie! Perhaps a bit more oomph next time, all right?" Ms. Dana consulted her clipboard. "All right, next I want to see the Emcee and the singing waiters onstage for 'Tomorrow Belongs to Me.' Hurry! We must get used to switching scenes quickly. Remember, our dress rehearsal is the day after tomorrow, and you're going to have to be quick quick quick!"

Derek leaned toward me as we hurried backstage. "Once we get to the dress rehearsal, maybe she'll let us do the scenes in the right order," he murmured into my ear.

I smiled. "Good point."

"Thank you." We were backstage now,

and he spun me toward him, planting a quick kiss on my forehead. "I'll be right back. I told the guys I'd help carry the new backdrop in from the hallway."

As he hurried off, Jenna Paolini wandered past, yanking at the hem of her very short skirt. Even though this wasn't technically a dress rehearsal, most of the Kit Kat Girls had been practicing in their costumes for the past few days.

"Lucky lucky," she hissed at me with a grin. "If I'd known the leading lady got that kind of bonus, I'd have tried harder for the part!"

I smiled as she rushed on past. It was hard to believe I was the object of envy for someone like Jenna. In fact, my whole life was pretty hard to believe at the moment. The past few days had been a whirlwind of dating my leading man—who also happened to be the man of my dreams.

Or is he? my brain piped up before I could stop it.

Shut up! the rest of me told it.

Still, I couldn't help wondering, though I wasn't quite sure why. Things were great between me and Derek so far. Ever since that kiss in the park the previous weekend, I'd even been able to speak and interact with him like a human being. In fact, getting to know him better had only confirmed that he was just as smart, funny, charming, and generally perfect as I'd always thought he was. So now that I had everything I'd always wanted, why was I already doubting it?

"Coming through!" I jumped as there was a commotion behind me. Scooting out of the way just in time, I watched as Derek, Tommy, Gary, and Nico came staggering into the backstage area carrying one of the show's huge painted backdrops.

Derek winked and smiled at me as he passed, but I just smiled back distractedly. Seeing Nico made my stomach clench a little. The two of us still hadn't talked about what had happened at his gig. In fact, we hadn't really talked at all.

I watched Nico as he set down his end of the backdrop and headed for the side door. He didn't meet my gaze or even glance over at me, even though he had to know I was there. I bit my lip, feeling as if I might cry. Why did he have to be so stubborn? Why couldn't he understand that I hadn't meant to hurt him? After all, he seemed to understand everything else about me. . . .

"Miss me?" a voice said into my ear, making me jump. When I turned around, I saw Derek grinning at me.

I smiled back. "Tons." I tilted my chin up as he came in for a kiss.

It's just the play, I told myself as we made out. *Rehearsals are almost finished, and we're all crazed and nervous. . . . Once the show is over and things settle down, I'll be able to get back to normal, make up with Nico, and get on with enjoying my dream-come-true life.*

"So what's the problem?" Calla asked, looking confused.

I shrugged and stared down into my half-eaten bowl of Ben & Jerry's. We were at Calla's house after rehearsal, recharging with a little snack before tackling our homework. The musical would be taking up pretty much all our time for the next five days straight, so we wanted to get as much schoolwork out of the way now as possible. While we ate, I'd told Calla about my latest weird doubts about me and Derek.

"I have no idea," I said. "All I can figure is maybe I'm afraid of being *too* happy or something. Or maybe it's just that I still don't quite believe this is real. I mean, why would someone like Derek actually want to go out with someone like me?"

"Is Derek doing anything to make you feel that way?" she demanded. "Is he acting like he's doing you a favor, or like he's too good for you?"

"No! Definitely not." I sighed and smiled, thinking about the way he looked at me. "He treats me like a queen."

"Then stop being so freaking insecure!" she scolded, shaking a finger in my face. "It's all in your head."

I looked down again, stirring the chocolate sauce at the bottom of the bowl. "You know me," I said. "Insecure is my middle name."

"Only if you let it be. Just remember, the only one who can make you feel insecure is *you*." She blinked, pausing with her spoon halfway to her mouth. "Hey. You know, I'm brilliant."

"I know." I grinned at her. "And you're right. I should stop second-guessing this thing with Derek and just enjoy it. That's what I keep telling myself."

She lowered her spoon and stared at me. "Yeah," she said slowly. "And *I* should stop feeling bad 'cause I'm not a size two."

"Oh! Um, yeah?" I agreed uncertainly. Calla and I hadn't really talked about her problem since that day in the car. "I mean, what do you mean?"

"I mean I've been incredibly stupid." She shook her head, looking amazed. "Think about it. That's the whole point of my character in the show."

"Being incredibly stupid?" I said dubiously. "I don't think Fraulein Schneider is—"

"No!" She laughed out loud, waving her hands. "That's not what I mean. I mean Fraulein Schneider and Herr Schultz let what other people thought of them ruin their lives, right?"

Now I saw what she meant. In the show, the couple wants to get married. But in the end they decide not to because Herr Schultz is Jewish and Fraulein Schneider isn't, and they're afraid of what people will think, especially with the Nazis gaining more and more influence all around them.

Calla grimaced. "Isn't that what I'm doing too?" she said. "I mean, so what if Glenn—or anybody else—thinks I'm too fat to play a love scene? It's their problem, not mine. I can choose to let it affect me, or I can just do my thing and have fun."

"That's right," I said loyally. "You're perfect just the way you are."

She chuckled and picked up her spoon. "Let's not get carried away here. We both know I could stand to lose a few." She stared at the ice cream dripping off the spoon. "And maybe I'll do something about that at some point. But if I do, it needs to be for *me*. Not because of what my costar might think when he puts his arms around me, or what other people might think when they see me up onstage." She grinned and winked. "Larger than life."

I smiled back, still wishing she'd let me try to help more, but proud of her for figuring things out on her own. "Great," I said, scooping up another bite of Cherry Garcia. "Now that you've figured out how to accept yourself and appreciate your own gifts and all that other Oprah stuff, how about helping me figure out how to accept and appreciate *my* big, handsome, amazing gift? Then maybe we can all get on with living happily ever after."

Nineteen

Our dress rehearsal was as crazy, horrible, and wonderful as dress rehearsals always are. On the negative side, Nico still wasn't talking to me, one of the singing waiters had caught a cold, and Lizzy Paolini broke a heel on her high-heeled dancing shoe. But that was okay. The shoe got fixed, the singing waiter took some Robitussin, and I had already vowed to force Nico to listen to my apology at the cast party after our final performance and was trying not to worry about it in the meantime.

There were some major positives too. Derek looked amazing in his old-fashioned suit. Someone ran in to tell us all three performances were already sold out. And best of all, Calla's revelation had broken her out of her funk once and for all. She laid down an absolutely incredible performance as Fraulein Schneider. Even Glenn seemed a little overwhelmed by her power and earthy charisma as she sang, danced, and acted her sizable butt off.

"You're a superstar!" I exclaimed as we both stepped back after the final bows, turning and grabbing her for a hug. "Congratulations!"

"Thanks, sweetie." Her eyes danced as she pulled back and planted a kiss on each of my cheeks. "You weren't too shabby yourself. Let's just hope we didn't just curse ourselves by being so good tonight."

I laughed, knowing she was referring to the old theater superstition that a terrible dress rehearsal meant a great performance and vice versa. But the giddy smile froze on my face as I glanced down into the orchestra pit. The band, a group of talented musicians drafted from the school's music department, was finishing up their final musical flourishes. Nico was directing them, and seeing him do his thing gave me a serious pang. What was it going to take to make him forgive me?

Cast party, I told myself. *You'll make it right with him at the cast party. Until then, don't let it throw you.*

But by opening night, my fight with Nico was still nagging at the edges of my mind. So were my worries about Derek. Why couldn't life ever be simple and straightforward, the way it was in my fantasies?

"Ready to go?" Ms. Dana asked, rushing around the cafeteria, where the makeup team was getting us actors ready. "Break a leg, Maggie!"

"Thanks." I waited for the sophomore girl who was doing my makeup to put the finishing touches on my eyeliner. Then I thanked her, got up, and rushed out of the room, doing my best to push all my worries out of my mind. It was showtime!

Outside the cafeteria door I almost bumped into Nico, who was racing down the hall in the direction of the music suite. "Oh!" he blurted out, skidding to a stop.

I stopped too. Or tried to, anyway. Unfortunately my high-heeled dancing shoes didn't want to cooperate and slipped a bit on the tile floor. I wobbled precariously, and for a second I was afraid I was going to give the phrase "break a leg" a whole new meaning. There was really no choice but to catch myself by grabbing onto Nico's arm before I wiped out.

It worked, and I stayed upright. But he jumped back as if I'd stabbed him. "Excuse me," he muttered, hurrying off without another word.

I scowled after him, fists clenched at my sides. Calla happened by, busily adjusting the waist of her housecoat, and saw me.

"What's wrong?" she asked breathlessly.

"Nothing. It's just Nico." I frowned. "He's so freaking *stubborn*! Why does he have to be like that? Especially tonight of all nights?"

"Brush it off, sweetie," Calla advised. "You've got a show to do."

"Yeah, you're right. Come on, let's go." I couldn't resist one last glare in the direction Nico had gone, but then I turned to follow Calla. The show must go on.

Maybe getting mad at Nico was just what I needed to add a little extra fire to my performance. Because that night, I truly *became* Sally Bowles—passionate, filled with energy and hope and desire, ready to pour my heart out for my art and the man I loved. From the moment I stepped onstage, I owned the part. It was amazing. From the opening number through my final song, the show seemed to pass in the blink of an eye.

The whole auditorium erupted with applause as we all stepped out for the curtain call. I joined hands with the rest of the cast for one big bow, then stepped forward to take my bows—first alone, and then hand in hand with Derek. Between bows, he gave my hand a squeeze and turned to wink at me. I smiled back, but my gaze kept wandering toward the orchestra pit. It was hard to see past the stage lights, but I kept trying to catch a glimpse of Nico. More than anything, I wanted to see what he'd thought of my performance.

No, scratch that. That wasn't what I was really after—a dispassionate critique by my singing coach. What I was really thinking about, I realized with a sort of weird twist of my gut, was celebrating my triumph . . . with Nico. Not Derek, but Nico.

I glanced at Derek beside me. He was blowing a kiss out toward the audience, mouthing the words "love ya, Mom!" Sweet.

As always, he looked impossibly handsome, and my heart swelled when he caught me staring and blew a kiss to me too. I smiled uncertainly, trying not to steal a peek toward the orchestra pit to see if Nico was watching, completely overwhelmed by my own feelings, even if I wasn't exactly sure what they meant.

Then it was all over, at least until the next night's performance. I was swept back-stage with the others, and there was the usual hugging and crying and congratulating for a while. Finally I peeled myself away, needing to catch my breath and just take it all in for a moment. After quickly changing out of my costume, I wandered out front to see who was out there in the audience. My parents weren't coming until the follow-ing night, but I knew some of my teachers, neighbors, and non-Thespian friends would probably be there.

"Maggie! Marvelous job tonight, child," a familiar voice called to me as I stepped into the auditorium.

I gasped and wheeled around. "Mr. Fayne! You made it!" I cried.

He beamed at me, looking a bit thinner than I remembered but otherwise exactly like his old wonderful self. "I wouldn't have missed it for the world," he said, grasping my hand in both of his. "I'm so proud of you, my dear."

"Thanks." I smiled, drinking in the sight of him. So much had changed since I'd seen him last. Even though most of the change was good, the thought made me kind of sad.

He glanced around the place. "I must admit, I never thought to try a musical. But once I heard about it, I had no doubts you all could pull it off. You have a glorious singing voice, Maggie, and of course Calla is quite the natural."

I nodded and smiled. If he only knew how hard it had been for me to release that voice, or how much Calla had struggled for that "natural" performance! Then again, this was Mr. Fayne. He probably did know. He was like that.

He was still musing on the cast. "And then there's our Nico, of course," he said, snapping me back to attention. "What immense talent that boy has."

"Yeah," I blurted out before I could stop myself. "Too bad he's not more talented at letting people know what he's really thinking."

"Beg your pardon?" Mr. Fayne raised one eyebrow in his quizzical, expressive way.

That was all it took. Yes, I'm blaming the eyebrow. Just like that, the whole story poured out of me. Well, the short version of it, anyway. But Mr. Fayne is pretty sharp. He seemed to grasp the issue right away.

"I see." He stroked his beard. "So you are happy with Derek, your new boyfriend, but cannot stop thinking about Nico, who is supposed to be your friend but isn't acting much like one at the moment. Do I have the gist?"

"Uh-huh, pretty much." I stared at him, hoping he'd tell me what to do, direct me, as he'd done so often and so gracefully in the past. But he just smiled.

"Well, I've always said the stage is a place of special magic," he said. "The best plays and the finest actors can sometimes allow us to catch a glimpse beyond and beneath the fantasy to what is true and important. Of course, like much in life, this can be a challenge. But nothing worthwhile is easy."

Before I could even begin to figure that one out, Ms. Dana came barreling toward us. She was dressed in a shimmery gold dress and a big, weird matching hat, and was beaming from ear to ear. "Mr. Fayne!" she cried. "I'm so glad you could make it. . . ."

I stepped away, leaving them to chat. The auditorium was suddenly feeling a little too crowded, so I stepped back out the door into the much quieter hallway. I was just in time to see Derek emerge from the cafeteria at the far end.

"Maggie! There you are." He hurried toward me, grinning. "Man, that was such a rush! Like a touchdown and a homerun all in one. No wonder you guys are so into this acting thing! I'm so glad I tried out." Catching my hands, he pulled me closer. "But not only because of that. If I hadn't been in this show, I might never have gotten to know you—my gorgeous Sally Bowles."

He bent and kissed me. I sighed and melted into his embrace, as usual unable to resist swooning at his touch.

And why should I resist? My life finally matched my fantasies. It was following my own script. Derek O'Malley was crazy about me, and we were together, and everybody knew it. Happily ever after. This was everything I'd ever wanted.

Wasn't it?

Twenty

Call me a wuss. Because I decided to go with the flow and worry about all my weirdly vacillating feelings once the show was finished. After all, what if all my bizarre ping-ponging thoughts about Derek and Nico were just some kind of postperformance rush unrelated to reality? That wouldn't be too surprising, really. After all, I'd relied on Nico for so much for so long—was this just my brain's way of resisting change, knowing that it was all about to end?

Then again, maybe it was fear of success. Everything was going so well right now—the show, Derek. Was I trying to sabotage myself, afraid that I didn't deserve so much happiness all at once? I had to wonder, although thinking that way made me feel like I should sign up to be on some daytime talk show:

TALK SHOW HOST: And when did you realize you had this fear of success, Miss Tannery?

ME, *miserably*: When I acted like a psycho and broke up with my dream guy right before we were supposed to act opposite each other in our school musical.

TSH: Hmm, I see. And then what happened?

ME: First of all, it ruined the next two nights of the show. Instead of acting like we were falling in love, he kept glaring at me. He even tripped me during one of my dances, so I fell off the stage onto my head and got a concussion, and then my understudy had to take over . . .

TSH, *intrigued*: Please, go on!

ME: Then, to make things worse, when I tried to talk to the guy I *thought* I might possibly like instead, *he* told me I was totally

shallow and lame. He even wrote
a punk song about it.

TSH: I see. What is the song called?

ME: Uh, it's called "Maggie Tannery
is Shallow and Lame."

TSH: Catchy. Now, for the benefit of
our audience, we happen to have
a video of Ms. Tannery's head-
falling performance—let's roll the
clip for the entertainment of the
entire nation!

TALK SHOW AUDIENCE: Whoo-hoo!

ME, *cringing*: Nooooooo!

Fortunately, even in the midst of all my
angst, the next two nights of the show went
just as astoundingly and fabulously great as
opening night. Well, at least as far as the
audience could tell. As for me, each performance felt a little more crazed and desperate. Luckily that feeling worked for Sally
Bowles. In fact it was as if I *had* become
Sally, just like Ms. Dana was always urging,
and that I knew I might as well sing and
dance and have fun now, since something
Big and Bad and Horrible was coming as
soon as the lights went down . . .

Okay, maybe that's a little overly melodramatic, even for an actress like me. I wasn't really Sally, this certainly wasn't pre-war Berlin, and I definitely wasn't dealing with Nazis and such. Just my own wishy-washiness and questionable decisions.

Still, I couldn't help wondering what came next. Once the final curtain call was over and the cast party ended, where did that leave me?

With Derek, I reminded myself with some frequency. *Exactly where I've always wanted to be.*

The cheers and whistles of the audience were still ringing in my ears as I changed out of my costume in the girls' bathroom across the hall from the auditorium. This was it. The final performance had just ended, and just like that, my reign as Sally Bowles was over. I had the same mixed feelings of pride, nostalgia, and relief that I always did at the end of a play. But this time it was undercut with a sort of weird, unsettling dread. Nico still wasn't talking to me. And now, with the show over, would he ever see a need to do so again?

Why should he? I asked myself as I pulled on the skirt I planned to wear to the cast party at Bethany's house. *It's not like we ever had anything in common outside this play . . .*

My brooding was interrupted when several of the other girls from the cast burst into the bathroom. They were laughing and chattering in high, breathless, excited voices about the night's performance.

"Oh! Maggie," Jenna said when she spotted me. "You'd better get out there. Your leading man is waiting for you!"

She giggled and made a smoochy face. Her sister did the same, and most of the others joined in, giggling more wildly than ever.

I smiled weakly, not really in the mood. "Uh, thanks," I said, hurrying out of the bathroom.

Derek was leaning against the wall in the hallway just outside, hands in the pockets of his jeans. "Hey," he said, straightening up when he saw me. "You look great."

"Thanks." I knew his compliment was a bit of an exaggeration—I still had on most of my stage makeup, and my hair was a wreck. But that was the fun of a cast party. Everyone always showed up looking like they were still half in costume. Derek himself had smudged eyeliner around his eyes and a faded spot of rouge on each cheek. I could only imagine what his football buddies would say if they saw him. But he still looked as devastatingly handsome as ever as he leaned down to give me a kiss.

I kissed him back, a little of that Sally Bowles desperation creeping in as I grasped him tightly around the shoulders with both hands. This was what I'd always wanted— what I'd spent hours dreaming about for the past three years. Being with Derek. Having him kiss me. Kissing him back as if we'd never stop . . .

"Whoa!" Derek was smiling when he finally came up for air. "That was amazing."

I didn't answer. That's because I'd just noticed Nico standing a little way up the hall just outside the auditorium door. How long had he been there? I felt my cheeks going pink, wondering if he'd just witnessed that kiss.

Derek turned and spotted him too. "Nico, my man!" he called, raising one hand. "Excellent job tonight. All three nights, actually."

"Thanks. You too," Nico replied, stone-faced. He stared at me for a second, then turned away.

Fine. If there was a choice to be made here, it seemed Nico had already made it for me. So if that was the way he wanted to be . . .

"Ready to go?" I asked Derek.

"Ready as I'll ever be," he responded easily.

At that, I felt a weird moment of déjà vu. Where had I heard him say that before? Then I remembered—I hadn't. It was one of the lines from Calla's script, one that he was supposed to say but hadn't. I half smiled, recalling that awkward encounter. Getting together with Derek had certainly had its ups and downs. Then again, nothing worthwhile in life was easy.

Especially when things go off script, I thought, shooting another glance at Nico as he disappeared back into the auditorium.

"Having fun?" Derek said into my ear.

I glanced up and nodded, not even bothering to try to answer him over the noise of the cast party. It was extra loud in Bethany's living room thanks to her dad's superpowered sound system, which some of the guys had cranked up to top volume. The glass doors were open to the pool area out back, and a few people were splashing around in the shallow end despite the cool night air.

"Come here." Derek took me by the hand and pulled me off the couch. "I want to talk to you for a sec."

I allowed myself to be pulled, realizing that maybe I wasn't the actress I thought I was. Ever since arriving at the party, I'd been trying to pretend to have a good time. But it wasn't working. For one thing, I was totally distracted by the fact that Nico had never showed up. I felt bad about that, knowing his absence was almost certainly my fault. But was that all I was feeling—guilt? Or was there something more to it?

Snap out of it, Tannery, I chided myself as I followed Derek outside across the pool area and through a little gate into the quiet, grassy backyard beyond. *You're wasting what should be one of the best nights of your life.*

Once out of range of the stereo, I could hear a few crickets or frogs or something chirping away in the late-spring night. They sounded kind of sad to me somehow, as if they were calling out for something they'd never find.

Yeah. I *really* needed to snap out of it.

"Hey," I said, tilting my head back to look up at Derek. "Um, what did you want to talk about?"

"I'm not sure." He peered down at me, his adorable face troubled. "I just feel like you're not all here tonight, you know? The past few nights, actually. Is anything wrong? Did I say something stupid, or accidentally insult your mother, or something like that?"

"No," I said. "Um, not really. I mean, sort of. Not. I mean, not, you know, the insulting thing. But I don't know . . ."

Great. Was I reverting back to my old, tongue-tied self?

I glanced around the darkened yard, looking for help. Then I realized what I was really looking for—or rather, *who* I was looking for. Nico. I was still looking for his help, even now that the show was over, even after all that had happened. Was I nuts?

No. Not nuts. Just maybe a little deluded.

Derek was still gazing at me with concern. "Listen, Maggie," he said, taking my hand in his. "You can talk to me. What's up? Are you bummed because the show's over or something?"

"No, it's not that." I took a deep breath. My whole body started trembling, and I suddenly felt like I might throw up.

Chick vomit is hot! I heard in my head, making me smile.

No. Stop it. I had to snap out of it and do what I suddenly knew I needed to do. Why hadn't I seen it before? Maybe I'd been so caught up in my dream-come-true fantasy that I'd lost touch with reality. Go figure, right?

"Maggie?" Derek said.

"Derek, I—I'm sorry. You're such an amazing guy, but I—I don't think we should, you know, be together. I—I—I think I might like someone else."

The last part came out all in a rush. Derek looked startled.

"Oh," he said, dropping my hand. "I see."

"I'm really sorry," I said, tears coming to my eyes. But not for Derek, not really. I was crying for all those fantasies. The stuff I'd thought I wanted. "You've been really great . . ."

There was a little more after that. But why belabor it? After all, a good drama always skips the unnecessary details. Suffice it to say that Derek handled it like the champ he was, thank goodness. He truly was a fantastic guy. Too bad it had turned out he wasn't the guy for me after all.

Anyway, soon enough Derek had melted back into the crowd at the cast party, leaving me standing there all alone in the dark yard feeling queasy and anxious and weirdly proud of myself all at the same time. I didn't know what would happen next, and I'd never been that great at improv. Would Nico listen to me? Would he give me another chance? I had no idea. I only knew I had to try. All my earlier annoyance and anger with him had dissipated, replaced by stomach-clenching anxiety and, well, let's call it sheer terror.

I headed back inside to find Calla, planning to ask if I could borrow her car to drive over to Nico's house. She wasn't in the noisy living room, so I wandered out into the front hallway. It was deserted out there and I stopped and leaned on the stairway railing for a moment, appreciating the quiet. Well, the relative quiet, anyway. The party still raged on in every direction, but at least there in the hallway I was somewhat out of range of most of the noise. As I stood there, the front door opened and a familiar figure came slinking through, hands shoved in pockets and head down.

"Nico!" I blurted out, hardly believing my eyes. Talk about arriving right on cue!

He glanced up at me, then frowned and turned away as if to hurry into some room off to the side where a bunch of people were watching TV. The wussy part of me was ready to let him go, then run off and whine to Calla and Duane, or maybe to find Derek and beg him to forgive me and forget what I'd said. . . .

But no. I wasn't going to be that Maggie anymore. At least not now, when it mattered way too much to wimp out. So I marched right up to Nico and grabbed him by the arm.

"Listen, we need to talk," I said firmly. Well, as firmly as I could manage, anyway, which meant that my voice shook only a little.

He yanked his arm away. "I don't think we have anything to talk about," he said, glancing around, clearly looking for Derek. "You don't want to keep Mr. Leading Man waiting, do you?"

I shrugged. "Actually, I just broke up with him."

"You . . . you did?" I could see that I'd broken through Nico's mask of grim indifference. He looked surprised and kind of confused. "Um, okay . . ."

"Yeah, I did." I swallowed hard. "See, I realized he wasn't the right guy for me after all. I thought he was for a while, but I've come to see that I was wrong. There's only one guy involved in this musical that I want as my real-life leading man. And that's you." I paused. "For what it's worth."

He stared at me for a long, long, looooooong moment. I held my breath, wondering if I'd read him wrong after all. What if that song wasn't really about me at all? What if Calla had been full of it when she'd said he liked me? What if I'd just broken up with Derek for no reason? What if, what if, what if . . .

"Wow." Nico cracked a smile for the first time in what felt like forever. "That was awesome. I can't believe you got that whole dramatic speech out without getting tongue-tied or working off a script. I'm proud of you!"

"What?" I blinked. Whatever reaction I'd expected, this wasn't it. Then again, that was just like Nico—keeping me on my toes.

He looked sheepish. "Sorry," he said. "Guess that's not what I was supposed to say right now, was it? See, I'm not real good at this guy-girl stuff. That's why I tried to talk to you before the only way I knew how."

"Yeah. You mean the song, right? I got that. It just took me by surprise, that's all." I bit my lip. "I guess I didn't handle it that great."

"No, it was totally my fault!" he said quickly. "I mean, yeah, I guess I'd sort of pictured how it would turn out in my head." He grimaced. "Only in real life, it happened kind of, you know, differently."

I could hardly believe my ears. It seemed I wasn't the only one with delusional day-dreams.

"Anyway, I'm sorry." He shrugged and slid me a sidelong glance. "Guess I kind of messed things up."

"Guess we both did." I gave him a tentative smile. "Anyway, I never had anyone write a song for me before. Could you . . . will you . . ."

He swallowed hard and met my gaze full-on. The laser beams were back, boring into me as if trying to read my innermost thoughts. I held my breath, not daring to speak or even move.

Then he gave that little grimace-smile of his, cleared his throat, and started to sing: "I know a girl, a talented girl . . ."

I felt my whole body relax as I realized what this meant. "So you forgive me?" I asked when he finished the first verse of his song. *My* song. "We're okay?"

"Yeah. Definitely okay." He hesitated, suddenly looking a little shy. "Um, so does this mean, you know . . ."

I smiled. "Yeah, you're definitely almost as bad at this as I am," I said. "Guess that means we're perfect for each other."

Before he could respond, I grabbed him by both hands, pulled him forward, and kissed him. It felt nice. And by the way he kissed me back, I had a feeling the two of us were going to be making beautiful music together for a good long while.

And as it turned out, I was right. But I won't get into that. After all, the best plays always end right at the beginning of the happily-ever-afters.

CURTAIN DOWN

About the Author

Catherine Hapka has written more than one hundred and fifty books for children and young adults. In addition to reading and writing, she enjoys horseback riding, animals of all kinds, gardening, music, and traveling. She lives on a small farm in Chester County, Pennsylvania, with a couple of horses, three goats, a small flock of chickens, and too many cats.

The next morning Kate stood outside her house with her duffel bag by her side. She'd been packed for weeks and couldn't stand the wait for even one more moment. Alexis had planned to pick Sierra up at her house, and then they would head to Kate's before motoring off to the west in Alexis's little green Ford.

Kate stood in her driveway, growing agitated for no reason at all. She had come outside more than ten minutes before her friends were supposed to get there, and she couldn't blame them for the fact that she was still waiting. She reached into her bag to grab her cell phone to check the time and realized it wasn't there.

Crap. She'd left it plugged in overnight and had forgotten to grab it from the kitchen counter before she'd locked up. She pulled out her keys and let herself back in—the phone was right where she'd left it the night before.

She had six new text messages and a voice mail. Before she could look at her messages, she heard Alexis's horn sigh in her driveway. The horn sounded like a dying cow sucking its last breath, and Kate chuckled as she slipped her phone into her pocket and hurried out the door.

Sierra waved to her from the front seat, and Alexis leaned her head out the open driver's side window. "I'm driving first shift so I can control the tunes, yo."

"You can drive every shift, babe. I will man the navigation." Kate swung her bag into the trunk and moved around to the back door. She stopped short when she realized the backseat wasn't empty. "What are you doing here?"

Sprawled across the backseat, one foot lounging into Kate's space, was Adam. He was drinking a bottled Frappuccino, and a little bit spilled as he shifted to make room for her next to him. Kate leaned into the window to glare at Alexis. "What is he doing here?" The panic was evident in her voice.

"Dude, why didn't you call me back?" Alexis swiveled in her seat. "I called you last night, and texted you, like, eight million times."

"I didn't get the messages." Kate was staring at Adam suspiciously. His precious soccer ball sat in his lap, taunting her. Her skin crawled at the memory of what had happened the previous afternoon. "Does anyone want to tell me what's going on?"

Adam put on a fake smile and—in a ridiculous Valley girl accent—said, "Like, I'm coming with you!" He clapped. "Road trip with the girls!" His face turned expressionless. "Yes, that's right, Kate. You and I will enjoy the magic of each other's company for the next"—he looked at the clock on the dash of the car—"one hundred twenty-six and a half hours in this car—approximately."

Kate shot a desperate look at Alexis, who glanced in the rearview mirror and then said, "Adam has a scholarship interview at the University of Michigan. He has to be there on Monday afternoon, and Aunt Michelle can't leave until Sunday. My parents knew we were planning to stop to see Kevin in Ann Arbor anyway, so they made me bring him with us. They insisted he didn't need to take the skanky bus when we were going to the exact same place."

Sierra leaned her head out the window. "Come on, Kate, just get in." Kate scowled at her before reluctantly sliding into the open spot next to Adam.

"I may have come across as genuine a few moments ago, when I jumped for joy about this road trip." Adam adjusted his position so he was taking up as much of the backseat as was humanly possible. "But let me tell you that I'm looking forward to crashing your road trip just slightly less than you ladies are looking forward to having me here. But fate aligned and brought us all together, so I think we should make the most of it."

Alexis rolled her eyes and signaled to turn onto the interstate. They were on their way. All four of them. As Kate turned to look out the back window to watch their hometown shrink into the distance, Adam said, "So, who wants to play truth or dare?"

When they stopped at a gas station in the middle of Pennsylvania for toilets and treats four hours later, Kate was convinced that she had died and gone to hell. Absolutely everything she had envisioned for their girls' road trip had soured into a giant disappointment.

Alexis was snippy (she refused to wear her glasses, and straining to see highway signs had given her a headache); Sierra was distant and quiet (Kate knew her parents' split was bugging her, but Kate couldn't talk to her about it with Adam lurking around); and Adam was rude, sarcastic, and condescending (translation: asshole). As far as Kate was concerned, the start of their highly anticipated road trip had been four of the worst hours of her life. She'd spent most of them folded into her corner of the car, trying to put as much distance as possible between her body and Adam's.

"Only one toilet works, so we'll have to flip to see who gets to test the waters." Adam was swinging a giant rubber fish with a key attached to it. He had been sent inside the gas station to find out where the loo was located. "I, personally, am relieved that I stand to pee."

"I'll go first." Kate rolled her eyes at Adam and grabbed the limp fish from his hand. "I brought seat covers."

"Of course you did." Sierra laughed. "I'm coming with you."

"Me too." Alexis grabbed Kate's hand. "See ya, Adam. Girls pee with partners."

When they were safely out of earshot, Alexis blurted out, "What's with you, Kat?"

"What do you mean?" Kate pulled out a tissue to open the door to the bathroom. The knob was grimy, and pieces of the tissue stuck to the metal when she twisted her hand away.

"I mean, why are you being so abrasive to Adam? What's your deal with him?" Alexis held the door open, and Sierra and Kate followed her into the restroom. The smell of cigarettes and sanitizer was overpowering. The size of the room made the disgusting toilet cowering in one corner look miniature. There was a machine on the wall dispensing Purple Passion condoms, and next to that was a wooden sign that said WOMEN ARE LIKE FISH: THE BIGGER, THE BETTER.

"My deal is he bugs me. He's rude, arrogant, and is ruining our road trip."

Sierra held her hand out for a seat protector, which Kate proudly pulled from her bag. "Ladies, turn away. I'll go first." Sierra laid the thin piece of paper over the toilet seat and groaned when it soaked up little wet puddles that had been camouflaged on the black seat. "This is disgusting—I'm squatting."

Alexis and Kate turned to face the condom machine to give Sierra some privacy. Alexis nudged Kate's foot with her own. "So you're saying that you are already convinced you're going to have a crap time on this trip, just because Adam is here?"

"Do you feel like things are off to a great start?"

"No, but I think that's because—" Alexis cut off as Sierra flushed the toilet with her foot.

Sierra piped up from behind them. "Because you're being a brat, Kate. Do you need to be so argumentative? I mean, he asked if anyone was hungry this morning, and you told him you'd rather starve than share his bag of pretzels. That's just sort of mean. I know he's not your favorite person, but maybe you could give him a chance, and see if things could be a little more . . ."

"Fun for everyone?" Alexis finished.

"So now it's my fault that our *girls'* road trip is ruined?" Kate couldn't decide if she wanted to scream or cry. How could her friends not see her side? "You're saying that since I think Adam is annoying, I'm the one ruining the trip?"

Alexis moved toward the toilet for her turn. "God, this is gross. No, Kat, that's not what we're saying. I guess I'm just wondering why he bothers you so much. You're not usually like this, and he's not *that* unbearable."

"You know I've hated him since middle school. And now he's always just such a prick that I can't really get past it. Lex, I can see why you deal with him—he's family. But, Sierra, doesn't he get under your skin?"

"Come on, Kate." Sierra washed her hands in the filthy sink, lifting her long, slender leg up to turn the faucet off with her flip-flop when she'd finished. "You know I don't let him bother me. He actually sort of cracks me up, if you want to know the truth."

"Dude, how did you do that?" Alexis was referring to Sierra's leg-faucet trick. "Kat, maybe you're just being a little bit dramatic? I've forgiven Adam for the Barbie doll rumor. You should too."

"I'll do my best to be civil," Kate said as she moved to take her turn at the toilet. "But I can't promise anything. I don't like when people mess with my friends, which he did, and you guys are just going to have to deal with that. I'll try to get over it, but unless he starts to act less like the asshole that I'm certain he is, then this car ride will be a little hostile."

Want to hear what the Romantic Comedies authors are doing when they are not writing books?

Check out **PulseRoCom.com** to see the authors blogging together, plus get sneak peeks of upcoming titles!